The Gilpin Girls

Jane Carver

THE GILPIN GIRLS
Copyright © 2023 by Jane Carver

ISBN: 979-8-88653-157-2

Melange Books, LLC
White Bear Lake, MN 55110
www.melange-books.com

Published in the United States of America.

Cover Design by Ashley Redbird Designs

Dedicated to Anna-Maria P. Cornell.
Sister of the heart

Special thanks to my editor, Jenna Katz, and Ashley Redbird
of Redbird Designs for a fabulous cover.

Chapter 1
When A Logical Decision Isn't

"Sometimes in life, we make decisions that seem quite logical at the time, and then we realize later that they were quite illogical." Rebecca looked over her shoulder at her youngest sister, Hannah, while still holding Colleen's braid. "Illogical means the decision wasn't the best one after all, sweetheart." She turned back to braiding hair, getting her middle sister ready for bed.

"You mean like when Henry decided to jump in the lake to save Robbie McQuire?"

"Hannah!" Colleen exclaimed. "That was mean! Thinking of Henry and his drowning hurts Rebecca's heart." Colleen often dramatized things, but this time Rebecca knew she was correct. Thinking of Henry *did* hurt.

Suddenly, the patter of light running feet came toward Rebecca. A short body slammed into her side, and small warm arms hugged her middle so tightly she had to suck in a deeper breath.

"I'm sorry, Becca! I didn't mean to hurt your feelings."

The child sobbed into her sister's dressing gown, wetting the fabric with huge salty tears.

Rebecca dropped Colleen's braid and turned to take the little girl into her arms. "Hush now, Hannah. Yes, thinking of Henry hurts me a little now, but honestly not enough to warrant all these tears months later."

"But...but...Henry decided to save Robbie. And he drowned," the child wailed.

"Come with me." Rebecca led her sister back to the window seat, sat then pulled the girl onto her lap. She brushed Hannah's hair back and used a thumb to dry the tears that still rolled down full cheeks. "Henry had a kind heart. He loved us all and would never want us hurt. But he loved others as well. When he saw Robbie in trouble that day, he decided to try and save him. Yes, Henry couldn't swim well, but he wanted to help. That decision seemed logical to him at the time. Understand that?"

Hannah nodded, her head resting against her older sister's shoulder, while a perfumed late spring breeze wafted through the window.

"Only later did that decision prove to be what I called it... illogical. It wasn't the best idea after all, considering that Henry did save Robbie by pushing him hard enough to allow the boy to get ashore, though my poor darling tired so quickly he couldn't save himself." Rebecca looked up in an effort to keep a few stray tears from rolling down *her* cheeks. "What seemed right at the time turned out to be not such a good idea."

"But what if I decide—"

"Listen, sweetheart, we can't go through life thinking our every move could be our last one. Or even thinking that our choices could turn out to be wrong. We make decisions and live with the consequences, no matter what."

Hannah sat without a word, twisting the belt of Rebecca's dressing gown. "I suppose. But I miss Henry." Her words came softly, sadly. She and Rebecca's fiancé had become close friends and often allies in silly pranks on the older girls.

When Henry died, everyone mourned, but Rebecca often wondered—and now knew—that her baby sister, only seven at the time, missed Henry as a grown-up playmate. "We all miss Henry, dear. He died something of a hero, but that doesn't make his death any less painful. However, he's gone and only lives in our memories now. Someday, perhaps, another person will come along that we can love just as much." She kissed Hannah's head and stood her back on the floor. "Now let's all get to bed, shall we?"

Taking her sister's hand, Rebecca moved over to Colleen's side. The girl still sat at her dressing table, idly weaving hair ribbons together.

Rebecca stopped behind Colleen while holding Hannah's hand. Before she left, however, she caught sight of the three sisters in Colleen's vanity mirror.

"Mama would love a photo of us like this," she sighed.

Colleen snorted and scoffed, "Not in our nightgowns she wouldn't."

"No, that's true, but look, Colleen." She nodded in the mirror to their reflection.

Eighteen-year-old Colleen sat on the stool, elbow on the dressing table, her russet-colored braid draped over one shoulder.

"Sturdy, like Papa," Hannah commented.

"What?" Colleen gave her baby sister a frown.

"I think Hannah means you've solid bones like Papa. Not

delicate like Mama. Beautiful, just like Grandma Gilpin. She had hair the color of yours, and she was a lovely lady," Rebecca assured her middle sister.

"If anyone is delicate, it's you, 'Becca," Colleen said as she examined her twenty-year-old sister in the mirror. "Like Mama."

"Fragile, Papa says," Hannah added.

"Huh! There's not a fragile bone in that delicate body of our sister. She's tall and beautiful with all that brown hair and brown eyes. But there's steel in her. Papa would be the first to agree with that," Colleen said.

"And what about me?" the baby sister asked.

Rebecca leaned down and kissed the smooth forehead while Colleen watched. Colleen seldom expressed emotions and rarely showed them.

"You, my dear, are the best of both Mama and Papa with all that light-colored hair floating around you like a halo and those grass-green eyes. You're neither sturdy nor delicate. You are perfect just the way you are."

"Well, the Gilpin girls aren't going to be perfect or beautiful tomorrow if we don't get some sleep tonight," Colleen groused.

"True, sister. Come, Hannah." Rebecca pulled Hannah away from the dressing table with its revealing mirror, from Colleen's room with its pale cream-colored walls and autumn-colored bedding and pillows.

"Good night, dear. Sleep well." The oldest and youngest Gilpin girls left the middle daughter in her room and moved down the hall.

Rebecca pushed open the door to Hannah's room and ushered her to the pretty bed all adorned in shades of pink. "Off with your slippers and dressing gown." She checked that the tie at the end of her sister's braid still held the soft strands tight as the little girl's hair often slipped the bonds of restraint. "Now up you go. Prayers then off to sleep."

"God bless Mama and Papa. Bless Rags, and keep him away from the bunnies. Bless Colleen, though she teased me again today about my freckles. Bless Mr. Gordon, so he can grow lots of pretty flowers for Mama, and Mrs. Gordon can still cook the best-est meals. God bless Miss Borden, my teacher. She had a worrisome day today with Johnny Silar." Just about the time Rebecca thought of shortening her sister's prayers, the little girl asked her final and familiar blessing. "And bless Rebecca 'cause she takes care of us all. Amen."

Too many truths floated around Rebecca. She kissed her sister and left the room, with a head full of thoughts about actions and consequences.

Chapter 2
Taking Things into Account

Tucked into her wide bed beneath a summer quilt done in grays and mauves, Rebecca Gilpin again wondered about her life. Not that her life was bad. Just different. Money was not an issue.

Papa made a fortune in his travels, carrying jewels from sellers to buyers, appraising and suggesting jewelry settings that might best display his merchandise, often buying jewels in his own name, therefore pocketing more money for the family.

She never asked just how he handled his transactions, though she kept his books. She'd taken over that job when she turned twelve, after Papa's accountant died. Being so much brighter than most thought her to be, because of her mild and pleasant character, she worked better than the elderly accountant had.

For eight years now, she had run the business from Papa's office. When her father traveled, Rebecca made the decisions. As time went by, being so close to her father that she could almost think like him, her decisions succeeded more often than not.

Going to school never presented a problem for her either. Even traveling to a private girls' school by train each week in Greenville, then home on Saturday and Sunday, seldom interrupted her bookkeeping or dulled her business acumen. Rebecca enjoyed being out of that particular institution. She had planned to marry, but when Henry died, she remained at home, satisfied to maintain the house and her father's books.

Her papa had taught her how to write, and because he was her mentor, her family marveled at how similar their signatures were.

Being a savvy businessman, Robert Gilpin discussed that similarity with Rebecca when she turned sixteen.

"There are times, dear daughter, when I'm not here, and proper decisions must be made."

"Yes, sir. I understand." Rebecca did understand as she had conducted several transactions by telegraph and mail already, always telling her father about them as soon as possible. He lauded her take-charge ingenuity.

"In light of your business abilities, I think it would profit the family if you could also sign official documents that arrive here at home. I mean, our initials are the same. Who's to know that R. E. Gilpin isn't Robert Evan Gilpin, but instead Rebecca Eugenia Gilpin?"

He pulled several documents forward and pointed to the signature on each. Even on close examination, her signature looked like his.

"You've signed such documents for several years now. Any financial transactions that require my personal presence, for instance at the bank, would have to wait until I return from my travels, of course. What say you, daughter?"

Tucked into her bed with soft summer breezes fluttering

curtains on a moonless night, Rebecca questioned the wisdom of their arrangement. A decision that seemed logical at the time. One that seemed reasonable, without dire consequences. So far, their agreement had worked.

Keeping that agreement secret from her mother and sisters, though, tried her soul. She wanted her family to need her. She wanted the father she adored to value her. But if Rebecca were honest with herself, keeping such an agreement came down to lying to her family as well as Papa's fellow businessmen.

Robert Gilpin fascinated his wife and daughters. Standing just at six feet tall, with narrow hips and fuller shoulders, he wore his brown hair in soft waves that complimented his golden-brown eyes and the smooth mustache that the ladies in his family adored. He charmed them with his wit and stories of travel across the United States when he returned home to his wife and daughters near Celina, Ohio. His jewel business took him mostly to the northern states, but he also traveled to California. Papa often told his oldest daughter that the South was simply too poor yet to afford his kind of jewels and the jewelry that came from them. The southern states still reeled from the traumas of the Civil War, though the conflict between North and South had ended thirty years prior.

Upon reflection that evening, Rebecca realized that Papa collected acquaintances, but few bosom friends. Only a few families in their small community not far from Celina called Gilpin a close friend. She decided such thoughts best saved until she worked on her accounting books when a fresh mind and the need for a sharp eye allowed her to mull over such thoughts clearly.

———

Several days later, Rebecca handed a bill over to her father. "Papa, this transaction seems extravagant. This hotel bill from Chicago." He perused it thoughtfully before handing it back to her. Waiting for her father's explanation, Rebecca twirled the end of her long hair. Hair that her mother insisted couldn't be up in a proper chignon until she turned twenty-one, though she allowed Rebecca to pile the mass atop her head with a few strands hanging down.

"I treated several businessmen to a nice dinner with wine. I wanted them to purchase more of the Senton jewels than they had earlier that day."

"And were you successful?"

"Two men did request a second viewing of the jewels the next morning. I sold a stone to each."

"So this hotel bill includes your room and meals as well as this business meal?"

For some reason, Robert grew agitated. "Yes. This is the way business is conducted, daughter. I expected you to know that by now. You have paid such bills for years now." He walked with exaggerated haste over to a wingback chair next to the fireplace, which had a screen stretched across to block downdrafts in summertime. He pointedly flipped open the newspaper and proceeded to ignore his bookkeeper, in this case, his oldest daughter.

How odd, Rebecca thought. Papa usually talked out his problems with her. He took risks, and when he did, he let her know so she'd know to expect any odd financial repercussions. A large bill due to a hotel in Illinois did not warrant such behavior.

Add this to my list of things to ponder—after Papa leaves

the house today, she told the pen she wagged back and forth in her hand.

Papa's office, or study as Mama often called it, lay awash in softened sunlight. A rich dark red paint covered the walls, a very masculine color Papa often said. Bookshelves lined one side of the room, Papa's rolltop desk sat on the other, an oil painting of the Mama and his daughters hanging over it. Rebecca's desk sat before the wide window. The sun at her back, she contemplated Papa's attitude toward the innocent questions she asked. Contemplation, however, would not see the bills reconciled.

Now she had at least four hours in which to reconcile the books and financial obligations Papa incurred in his work and travel. The hours passed faster than she realized. At some point, Papa drifted from the room. Sometime later, Hannah came in, carrying a plate of cookies and two glasses of milk on a small tray.

"Colleen not joining us today, dear heart?" Rebecca left the desk and moved several books from the table between the two wing chairs.

"She said she would be late coming home. About thirty minutes. She needed to talk to Cherry Hall about something." Hannah set the tray down, one glass of milk wobbling enough that Rebecca rescued it.

"Can't have soggy cookies, can we?" She winked at her little sister and waved her to the chair across from her own. "What shall we drink to today, Hannah?" Her sister always had something positive to say about each day, even if the girl's notion of positive sometimes bordered on silly.

"School's out at the end of this week!"

"Oh, I say! That *is* cause for celebration." Rebecca raised her glass, while Hannah did the same, the younger girl holding hers with both hands. "To summertime freedom!"

"Here! Here!" Hannah approved the salute, and the two clinked glasses carefully before taking up a cookie each.

"How did your day go? Did Johnny give your teacher cause for trouble today?"

Rebecca listened closely as Hannah answered. She cared what her sisters thought and always tried to be kind about their adventures. Hannah resembled her in so many ways, Rebecca realized. Their other sister, Colleen, should learn such ways as Hannah had—trusting, cautious, docile yet flexible.

Colleen Amanda Gilpin is her own person, Rebecca thought with a sigh. Colleen wanted control of her own life, and that conflicted with her parents' desires for their daughters. Most times, Colleen remained levelheaded, but she seldom shouldered the blame if whatever she did went wrong.

For a second, Rebecca's attention drifted, and Hannah caught her woolgathering. "Are you listening to me?"

"I'm sorry, Hannah. My thoughts did wander for a second or two. It's been a long demanding day. I'm tired, that's all. Forgive me?"

"I forgive you."

"Thank you, sweetheart. Now—"

"I'm finished with my milk. I'll do my school assignments now." Hannah interrupted as she stood and gathered the tray with empty plate and glasses, which she habitually turned upside down, the better not to drop them on the way back to Mrs. Gordon in the kitchen. "Oh, and I ate your second cookie, though you didn't notice."

"You scamp." Rebecca reached for Hannah in order to toss her braids about her head, but the younger sister proved faster. Sweet laughter floated back to the office as she made her escape.

Chapter 3
Mama Joins the Family

The family sat at the dining table. Felicity Gilpin had joined them, though she often took her evening meal in her room. Born into an old New England family, Mama had not inherited her ancestors' robust health. After the birth of her last child, Felicity never recovered her vigor. Oft times the girls found their mother sunk into a sort of fog, near to a depression, that she seldom could shake off.

She looked like a fragile, pale queen, nothing like the mother of three children. She wore her hair—a lovely combination of russet, brown and white—atop her head with a large bow at the nape of her neck, much in the style that her daughters wore. Papa once told Rebecca that his wife was so delicate that a strong breeze would knock her over.

"How are you tonight, my dear?" Robert held his wife's chair as she glided into it, more wraith-like than human woman. The girls knew Mama would eat little. But they smiled to see her join them. Most time, they visited her in her suite of rooms on the second floor.

"I'm...better, Robert. I feel invigorated by the blooms Mr. Gordon has coaxed from the bushes in the garden."

The large three-story colonial home stood among tall oaks on twenty acres. The family enjoyed their privacy. A wide porch ran across the front of the house, providing shade from summer sunshine and shelter from winter storms. A front door with sidelights graced the middle of the first floor, while wide windows ran across the front of the first and second floors. Tall dormer windows in the attic provided means to vent fresh air through the house as well as storage.

Coming in the front, past abundant blooms of roses, a visitor would find the formal drawing room to the right. A wide hall led directly from the front door to the back. The staircase rose just left of the hall, and the smaller parlor lay to the left of that. Down the hall, beyond the stairs to the left was Papa's office and to the right was the formal dining room with the kitchen at the rear corner of the house. Each member of the family had his or her own bedroom.

At the rear, double doors opened from the kitchen onto a brick porch under another wide over-hang. Beyond that lay the blooms Mama referred to.

The garden behind the house, a massive gathering of flowers, bushes, and century-old oaks, was Mama's delight. Before her descent into despondency, she had often worked beside Mr. Gordon, pulling weeds, planting flowers, and clipping branches. The old man thought it not proper, but he could never dissuade Mama. Blooms from the Gilpin garden had graced tables and sideboards as well as each bedroom. While the flowers hadn't been as numerous within the house for years now, those blooms still filled the air with sweet scents and delighted the eyes with beauty outside.

Rebecca watched her mother closely for signs of fatigue,

but this particular night, Felicity did indeed seem better. While Mama avoided stressful situations now, in times gone by that only Rebecca could remember clearly, her mother had coped with change, though she did not care for it. She believed strongly in family ties. To Felicity, her daughters and husband were the center of her world. She depended on Robert for everything, each choice and decision. When he traveled, Mama leaned on Rebecca.

Mama one day will fade away, leaving us with a ghost at the foot of the table. That reminded Rebecca of the question of Papa's friends and acquaintances. Papa attended Mama carefully, lovingly. But he never seemed to miss her as much as she missed him. How odd! Rebecca knew other couples so close that if one were to die, the other would as well from pure heartache.

Oh dear! Should I fade away because Henry died? I loved him. He loved me. But...

She turned her attention back to the family as Hattie, the maid, cleared the table of dishes and food.

"Life hands out problems so you can solve them," Robert Gilpin intoned solemnly. That was the tried and true motto he lived by.

"So Papa would say often when he returned from business trips," Rebecca said, throwing a wicked glance at her two sisters.

Colleen interpreted her sister's glance. "I remember."

"Me too." Hannah almost jumped in her chair in her enthusiasm.

Rebecca picked up the story, one eyebrow lifted, daring her father to say nay.

"Papa would sit quietly, listen to our concerns then stand. Solemnly he'd place a hand on the shoulder of the one with the gravest concerns, grasp his coat lapel with his other hand, lift his eyes as if seeking guidance from the Almighty, and intone that sentence. I was four when I realized Papa did this ritual each time he returned.

"After explaining my worries about a fat bee that threatened me each time I neared the peony bush in the backyard, Papa stood, laid his hand on my shoulder, secured his lapel, and opened his mouth. By the time he got to the word *problems* I was speaking with him, one hand on an invisible shoulder, the other holding an invisible coat lapel, my eyes lifted as gravely as his."

To her surprise and great delight, her mother's mouth lifted in a frail smile. The story might irk her father a bit, but it made her mother happy, so Rebecca was as well.

"And to make matters worse," said Colleen, "when I was about two, or so I've been told by Becca, I began copying them both. I remember I spoke as fiercely as I thought Papa often sounded. I assumed the same position Rebecca and Papa took and mouthed Papa's platitude in my baby garble."

"And I gasped to see my little darlings—both of them no less, later all three!—mocking me. I huffed and puffed for a full minute," Papa blustered.

"And then Papa broke into laughter that shook the windows," Hannah finished. "I love that most of all—Papa's laughter." Hannah clasped her hands together, as if her father's laughter was a great gift.

"I feared Papa would never forgive our offense to his guiding light of life. But even as he blusters, he laughs and winks, assuring us he still loves us." Rebecca sighed, knowing that as funny as their story was, her father took the credo he lived by deadly serious. Even Mama, with her fragile health and delicate beauty, emphasized often how important those words were.

"There's no problem the Gilpin girls can't solve." Papa's pride in each of his daughters was undeniable.

Rebecca looked around the table. Mama still smiled, but her strength had faded sometime during the story. Mama needed her bed. Papa nodded to Rebecca. That was his way of telling his oldest daughter to handle Mama. Papa would remain seated at the head of the table, as befitted the man of the house, sipping a brandy while caressing his mustache.

Rebecca patted her hair and nodded to Colleen. The two asked permission to leave the table. With another nod from Papa, they guided Mama up the stairs to her room, sat her on her vanity table's padded stool, and proceeded to remove her eveningwear then ease her into a nightgown.

Mama's room reflected her current state of health. Subtle mauve pink with cream curtains and bed covers. Flowers filled vases near daguerreotypes of the Gilpin and Callaway parents, the girls' grandparents.

"Sweet dreams, Mama." Colleen bent over and placed a soft kiss on her mother's cheek.

Mama barely noticed, her eyes focused somewhere beyond the room. Rebecca saw sorrow enter her sister's eyes as she lifted up from the bed. For all her rebellious ways, Colleen loved her mother deeply.

"Sweet dreams to you as well, sister." Rebecca laid a hand on Colleen's arm and held it there a few seconds.

Colleen nodded even as she glanced back at her mother who had fallen asleep just that quickly.

"I'll watch over her for a little longer. Get Hannah, and read to her, will you?"

"I will, but we both know she prefers your reading to

mine." Colleen gave her older sister a lifted brow but went quietly.

"Robert?"

To Rebecca's surprise, Mama awoke, her eyes on the door, as if waiting. "It's only me, Mama. Would you like me to read to you?"

"Robert? Where's Robert?"

"He's at the table with Hannah." Mama's mind seemed to wander.

"Will he come say goodnight?"

"I'll go ask if you'd like."

"Yes, please."

Assuring her mother that Papa would come up, Rebecca lifted her skirts and all but galloped down the stairs. She skidded to a halt just outside the dining room. Dropping her skirts, she entered the room and walked to the head of the table where her father now sat alone.

"Papa, Mama wants you to come up and say good night. She had a wonderful time with us, but I fear the activity drained her strength."

Her father sat still long enough that Rebecca wondered if he would come. Why hesitate, she asked herself.

"Please, Papa, if only for a few moments."

"Of course, daughter. Of course."

By the time they reached Felicity's bedroom, she lay asleep, breathing heavily. This time there would be no last minute request. Her strength gone for the day, she slept.

Rebecca closed the door carefully. "Maybe tomorrow, Papa."

"Yes, yes. Tomorrow."

Robert turned down the hall to his rooms, leaving his oldest daughter to ponder her parents' relationship.

———

Several nights later, Papa's credo came up again while the girls gathered in Colleen's bedroom. Rebecca tied each of her sister's braids, something she had done since Colleen was a wee girl. Hannah sat quietly while Rebecca twisted strands of Colleen's hair, one over the other.

"Hand me a ribbon, Colleen. I'm almost through," Rebecca said.

Colleen leaned forward, pulling painfully on her hair. She searched among the jars and boxes lying on her dresser but found no ribbon. "Loosen up a second, please." Her sister eased her hold, and Colleen rummaged through the drawers on both sides of the dresser. A frown marred her normally sunny face. She tossed a threat over her shoulder to her youngest sister. "Hannah, have you been in my ribbons again? If you have, I swear I'll warm your bloomers!"

Hannah sat quietly on the window seat, her attention focused on a large bumblebee buzzing at the edge of light cast through the window. Without turning her head, she answered in a calm voice that suggested she was more mature than her seventeen-year-old sister. "Why would I borrow your ribbon? I have plenty of my own. Besides, Rebecca used it the other night when Rags tore hers." Passing the problem from her slender shoulders to her older sister's, she went back to watching the bee, a frown of worry etched between her narrow brows.

"Rebecca, that true?"

"Oh dear. I'm afraid it is. Sorry, dear. I forgot. Here, hold this, and I'll get yours." Rebecca handed over the braid's tail end and dashed out of the room. In less time than expected— perhaps because she ran—she returned with the soft white length of ribbon. "Here it is. Rags shredded mine when we were playing tug. I saw yours lying on the bed stand and borrowed it." She quickly tied off the braid and patted her sister's shoulder. "I meant to return it. Honestly."

Satisfied that no one intentionally took her possessions, Colleen gave her sister a smile that lit her face. "No harm done."

"He's after me," Hannah said softly as if speaking louder would provoke attack.

"What did you say?" Colleen turned on her padded cushion.

"Who's after you, dearest?" Rebecca crossed the room, bent down and looked out the window with her baby sister. The bronze wire screen, a recent addition to the home, allowed the girls to look out without insects flying in, as they did when Rebecca and Colleen with little girls.

"Him." Hannah pointed to a bumblebee that hovered mere inches from her finger.

"That's a bumblebee, Hannah," Colleen affirmed.

"I know. He's been following me."

Rebecca sat beside her sister and slipped an arm around her shoulder. The child had yet to turn her gaze away from the insect. She refrained from laughing because the memory of a similar incident floated up to remind her that things like this were real to children. "Tell me what's happening that you think a bee is following you."

"I was playing by the peony bushes, and this bee kept following me. I couldn't make him go away." Hannah waved her hand, imitating her attempts to shoo the beast away. "And now he's followed me to the house." She shuddered and snuggled closer to Rebecca. "He scares me."

"Oh, for God's sake!" Colleen tossed up her hands and

flounced over to the bed where she threw herself back on the covers in dramatic fashion.

A gentle hug eased the little girl's shivers. "You do have a problem, don't you?" Rebecca stated the obvious. "The same thing happened to me when I was a little girl, much younger than you."

"How did you solve your problem?" whispered Hannah.

"My problem. My solution, dear. This is your problem. What would Papa say if he were here right now?"

"I'm gonna have to solve this on my own, aren't I?"

"Yes, you are. You're smart enough and old enough to do that." Rebecca smoothed the damp hair off her sister's forehead. "So now. What would Papa say?"

Hannah let out a deep sigh and finally turned from the window to face Rebecca. "Life hands out problems so you can solve them."

"That's right. Now, what is the solution to your problem?"

"Wonder if she'll come up with the same answer you did, Rebecca?" Colleen had turned on to her stomach and propped her head up on one hand. Her grin said she remembered the story of Rebecca and her bumblebee.

"Well," Hannah cut a glance over her shoulder to see that the bee still buzzed near the edge of darkness. "Maybe this isn't the same bee."

Rebecca nodded. "That's always a possibility. He may have simply been drawn to the light."

"But if it is the same one, then he followed me." Hannah leaned forward and waved a slender hand at him. "Go home. Go back to the peony bush."

As if the tiny creature understood her, the tiny insect streaked off into the night. All three girls gasped.

"I solved the problem!" Hannah crowed.

"At least you did here at the house. What about when you play by the bushes? What happens when he shows up there?" Colleen wasn't above guiding her sister with thoughtful hints.

"Maybe that's his home. And the flowers are his." Hannah leaned out the window, facing the enormous bush though the night remained without moonlight. "Perhaps I might stay away from the bush until it stops blooming. That way, he can have the bush and won't bother me."

"An excellent idea, little one!" Rebecca hugged Hannah and used the end of her own braid to tickle the youngster's nose. "Exactly the solution I came up with years ago."

"Problem solved!" Colleen vigorously thumped the bed cover in lieu of clapping.

"A Gilpin girl genius!" Rebecca shot her hand in the air, waving it like a flag proclaiming victory.

A problem presented; a solution discovered. No harm done.

Chapter 4
Not So Much a Lady

"I love summer!" Colleen tossed her head back and threw out her arms, her long hair coming free from the clasps that held it against the sides of her head. "Months and months of sunshine and free time. No more being cooped up inside. And today is the last day at Miss Marley's Finishing School. Such perfection." She blithely forgot her older sister's circumstances.

"Mama wants me to read to her each day," Hannah said as she scuffed her boots in the budding grass. "She says I don't have to take naps anymore, but my reading will improve if I read aloud." Her frown showed she didn't agree. "Why me?"

"I did it when I was your age and Colleen after me, dear. So don't complain. Mama doesn't get out, and she enjoys good stories. But her eyes are not strong like yours." Rebecca pointed out a fat crow walking the ground near them to take her sister's mind off the prospect of spending several hours each glorious summer afternoon shut inside with their mother.

The school bell had just begun ringing for the last time that year as the girls approached.

Hannah's shoulders drooped a bit until Colleen reminded her, "Last day of school, little sister."

"I know, and I'll enjoy the summer, really I will. But I'll miss Katy and Sarah. Their families are traveling to the South to visit relatives. They won't be back until the 4th of July. Then we can celebrate." Lost in her thoughts, Hannah then realized what she said and tossed a guilty glance at Rebecca. "I'm sorry, sister. I forgot about Henry."

The older girl put her arm around Hannah's shoulder and squeezed her tightly. "Don't worry about it, Hannah. I'll never forget him. But he's gone. My year of mourning is almost over. He'd be happy to see me out of this gray."

Colleen eyed her older sister up and down. "Certainly looks better than the black you wore for months. You would have thought you two were married instead of merely engaged."

"He deserved to be mourned, Colleen. I only wish his parents had remained. But I understand why they moved." She let the younger girls walk on a few steps as she stopped to admire the lake next to the road. Henry Lindsey had proposed to her next to that lake. She had accepted on its wide bank. Their families had celebrated the engagement at the Gilpin's home with a picnic on the back lawn and a magnificent view of the lake. But Grand Lake Saint Marys took Henry's life. The young man drowned July 4th the previous year. Rebecca's self-imposed year of mourning would end in six weeks.

"So many changes...so many. But none I expected," she murmured.

"Hey, Rebecca, you coming?"

"Coming, Hannah." She moved forward with determined steps, ready to wave her sister off to school then walk to town with Colleen.

"Remember last year? That was Colleen's last year here." Rebecca winked at Hannah. "Now she's wearing her hair up, and her hems are longer. Attending a finishing school...oooh. A regular lady, she is."

If there was one thing Colleen Gilpin was not, it was a lady. She was too blunt and honest. Too rebellious and unpredictable, according to her mother.

"A lady, huh?" Colleen gathered her skirts and leaned forward. "Bet I can beat you to the door, Hannah." Like the wind, Colleen pulled the books out of her little sister's hand and flew off down the path toward the open schoolhouse door.

"Hey, no fair!" Furiously, Hannah gathered her scattered books and tore off after Colleen. Rebecca was laughing too hard to run. She strolled sedately up the board stairs and greeted Miss Borden, the teacher, as her sisters panted on the front steps, debating who won.

"They pelted toward me like two racehorses. And now they sound like two nags," the teacher whispered as she and Rebecca laughingly shooed Hannah inside and waved Colleen back to the road.

———

Her bookkeeping finished early, Rebecca walked toward Hannah's school, ready to enjoy the early summer warmth after being in the office for hours. By now, Colleen should have walked from the finishing school in town back to

Hannah's schoolhouse. Hannah, of course, would exchange teary farewells with her bosom friends.

"Hi ho, sister. What are you doing here?" Colleen joined arms with Rebecca, while Hannah took hold of her hand. The trio set off for home.

"My eyes needed rest, and the sunshine is too wonderful to ignore, so I decided to meet up with you two as you journeyed home."

"A fine surprise, I say. Now if I had something to eat, the world would be perfect," Colleen cheerfully complained.

"How about an apple?" Rebecca reached into her skirt pockets and took out two apples. "I couldn't wait, so I ate mine while coming to meet you." She held one out to each girl.

"Humm, this is good," Hannah said with a full mouth, so her words came out muffled with apple bits. Then she swallowed and asked in a more understandable tone, "Any word from Papa today?"

"Not that I have heard, dear." Rebecca shortened her stride, pulling Colleen to a slower pace, when she noticed Hannah's downcast face. "But I expect him any day now." When Hannah's face brightened, Rebecca knew she'd said the right thing.

Like the best of friends that they were, they walked home in summer silence, satisfied with the way the world was at that moment. Rags, Mr. Gordon's dog, joined them as they drew closer to home. The mutt, however, deserted them at the front porch when he heard Mrs. Gordon rattling pots in the kitchen. The trio strolled across the wide green lawn and up the brick path in front of the white colonial.

When the girls stepped in the front door, they saw Hattie at the bottom of the stairs. Fair with freckles on her nose, she worked inside, while Charlotte and Peter Gordon were housekeeper, groundskeeper, and carriage driver. Short but lean and strong, Hattie's eyes twinkled, and her smile spread from ear to ear. She didn't have to say a word. The girls knew.

Papa was home!

They raced up the stairs in a flurry of petticoats. At the landing, Colleen pulled Rebecca's braid in order to get ahead. Tussling allowed Hannah to reach Mama's room first where she waited for her sisters.

"How much more perfect can this day get?" Colleen gasped as she swung around the newel post ahead of Rebecca. "Finishing school is complete, and Papa's home." Despite the haste of their journey to their mother's suite, the three calmed to a walk at the door. While their breath still came a bit fast, the glow on their cheeks said they were anxious to see their father. Their mother too, of course.

Hannah was the one who broke first, yanking the door-knob so hard that the great slab of wood fairly rattled in its casement. "Papa!"

She flew across the softly-colored room and flung herself into her father's arms. Luckily, he heard them coming and was standing. Otherwise, the three would have turned over the chair in which he sat moments before.

Mama clapped her hands, while her fairy-like laughter filled the spaces between giggles, hugs, and kisses.

"Oh, my darling daughters, I am so glad to see you," Papa said as he gathered his girls around him and sat back down. Rebecca sat on one arm of his wide wingback chair, while Colleen took up position on the other. That over-sized chair sat in Mama's room specifically for Papa's pleasure. As the baby of the family, Hannah sat in his lap. "I have missed you so."

He sighed and hugged Hannah as his older daughters draped loving arms over his shoulders. "My dear Felicity, you have gifted me with three angels." When his wife raised a delicate brow to question him—for she stayed at home with them and knew they were anything but angels—her husband expounded in mock gruffness. "Why just look here. They represent the very best of yourself, and you are an angel sent to earth to bring me joy."

Rebecca glanced over her papa's head at Colleen. "Papa does like to go on, does he not?"

When he blustered under her teasing words, she kissed his full head of brown hair, only lightly touched with gray at the temples.

"And how are our daughters like angels, sir, if one may ask?" Mama raised her feet to the small stool in front of her chair and arranged the light blanket over her lap. Her grin showed that she, too, teased.

This was one of Mama's good days, Rebecca decided.

"Each of our girls is bright and healthy. I would say they are geniuses, but then that would sound prideful. They are attractive and can look forward to beaus pounding on the front door. Rebecca is tall and slender with a charming smile and manner. Colleen," he paused for a second, "is a bonny lass with a quick wit. While our Hannah is a waif, who steals hearts even now. Your hair, my dear—" Papa waved a hand at his wife.

"What about my hair?" Mama rushed to pat a stray curl or two that tickled her temples. "Am I turning gray from worry, sir?"

"Nothing of the kind. But your hair has a touch of gold. And cotton white and feathery streaks of light brown. And just look here. Rebecca's hair is the warmest light brown." He reached up and tweaked his oldest daughter's braid. "Colleen's hair is quite as golden red as any sunset. Like her grandmother Gilpin's. While our darling Hannah here has hair the color of your cotton nightie."

All four ladies gasped at his reference to night clothes. "Really, Robert. Such words in front of the girls."

For a moment, Rebecca feared her mother might relapse into her mental fog after such a comment.

"Well, that's what they are! Nightgowns. Night clothes. Nighties." Robert repeated just the words just to aggravate his wife and girls. But he winked at his wife and patted Hannah's arm. "Soon enough, these young ladies will hear worse, I suspect. If not already at school. Hey, girls?"

Colleen and Hannah shot a look at Rebecca, waiting for her reaction.

Rebecca was no fool. She *had* heard worse behind the schoolhouse where the boys gathered to smoke while talking about girls. The blacksmith in the village had a tendency to cuss when a horseshoe didn't bend to his will. Even Peter Gordon tossed out the odd curse word now and then when weeds invaded his garden. But she wasn't about to admit that to her parents. Let them think their children's ears pure.

When no one said anything, Papa dropped the subject.

"Young ladies, for as beautiful and angelic as you are, I would spend a quiet evening with your mother." He smoothed his mustache while the look he bent on Mama set her to blushing, charm oozing out of him. "So off you go to your rooms. For this one night, I will ask Mrs. Gordon to bring you each a supper tray upstairs. Your mother and I shall dine in her rooms."

He stood, embraced his daughters, and whispered something to each, something important to only that one person. Something special.

"You are the rock of this home, my darling," he whispered to Rebecca.

The girls filed by their mother, kissed her ivory-colored cheek, and left the room, aware that Papa would quietly close the door, leaving the world to wait on them.

Papa's words were a compliment to be sure, but later in her room, she wondered why Papa didn't consider his wife the foundation of their home.

Chapter 5
A Charming Rogue, Perhaps?

S everal weeks later, Rebecca found the maid in a nervous state.

"Miss Rebecca?" Hattie stood at the bottom of the staircase and worried the newel post fiercely as if she had something important to say and waited impatiently for permission to speak.

"Yes?" Rebecca had planned on helping Hannah with her numbers but stopped when she saw how anxious the woman appeared.

"I just took the mail up to the Missus. Do it every day, then stay to dust her room while she reads. If anything needs doing, she tells me then."

Rebecca nodded. That routine hadn't varied since she could remember. She was sure it had been established when Mama and Papa bought the house.

"Only this time, I got a special delivery. A boy brought it. Missus opened a fat envelope and went all pale. Her hand went to her heart, and she glistened with sweat." Hattie's twangy New England accent broadened when she attempted to whisper. "I came straight to find you. The Mister went to the city at dawn and won't be home any time soon. Maybe you should...?"

The maid left her plea for help hanging.

When Robert Gilpin was away from home, all matters went first to Mama. Most often those same concerns fell into Rebecca's hands. Since she turned twelve, she had taken care of the household finances as well as being her father's book-keeper. No one thought it odd in the Gilpin home. No one outside the home knew. That's the way the family liked it.

Here was a problem that she would have to handle. Mama was too fragile to deal with a crisis.

Because the woman still stood on the step, now wringing her apron, Rebecca put on a determined face and patted the older woman's hand. "I'll just pop up and see what's worrying Mama."

"Oh, thank you, Miss." Hattie bustled off to the back of the house, not concerned that she'd dumped a predicament on the younger woman's shoulders.

Tucking Hannah's schoolbook in the crook of her arm, Rebecca made her way upstairs to her mother's rooms. Silence answered her knock. Afraid her mother might have swooned, she opened the door in time to see her mother's hopeful face lift to hers.

"Look." Mama held out a thick sheaf of papers in lieu of a greeting. When her daughter took them, she slumped in her wingback chair and twisted the curl by her ear, a sure sign Felicity Gilpin had no solution to the problem.

Rebecca perused the papers quickly. "This is a deed and requires an immediate signature. How did this come, Mama?"

"By special delivery. The boy is waiting in the kitchen to

take the letter to the post. The papers were delayed somehow. The due date is tomorrow. And this is the deed your papa's been waiting on."

Robert Gilpin traveled, bought, and sold. Rebecca once heard him referred to as a *speculator*, but the word offended her. Her father had been waiting for this deed for over a week. He had finally gone to Celina that day to check on the progress by wire. Somehow, he and the papers crossed paths. Now here they were, waiting for a signature and a hasty dispatch, and Papa was nowhere around.

"Mama, will Papa return soon?"

"I'm not sure, dear. He did mention catching the train to Dayton if he learned nothing in town. He may not return for a few days." Felicity paled more, her hands normally so still folded her gown into pleats. "What shall we do?"

"Calm yourself, Mama." Rebecca pulled the footstool close to her mother's chair and took her thin hands in her own. "Your hands are like ice. Let me warm them. I have a plan to save Papa's deed and good work here, but we must get you comfortable."

Rebecca's plan involved forgery on a grander scale than she had ever done.

"You have a plan?" The older woman sighed and slumped into her chair, a look of peace on her face that gladdened Rebecca's heart.

Not willing to leave her mother alone, Rebecca let out a sigh of relief when someone knocked on the door. "Come in."

Mrs. Gordon entered with a small tray with cup and teapot. "Pardon, Miss, but I was thinking the Missus might enjoy a cup of tea about now."

"Oh, Mrs. Gordon, you are a jewel. Mama is chilled, and that's exactly what she needs."

While the gardener, Peter Gordon, was a slight, balding man with a huge mustache, his wife, Charlotte, who now bustled around setting out the tea for Mama, was a more substantial person with a dour-looking face that belied a kind and compassionate heart.

Rebecca crooned to her mother, while Mrs. Gordon prepared a cup. "Here, Mama. Drink this, and let Mrs. Gordon stay until you are done. I'll take care of this." She patted the sheaf of papers in her lap.

"I have no idea what I would do without you, my dear." Mama reached for her teacup and thanked the housekeeper. She no longer appeared worried about the matter. Her daughter would take care of the situation.

———

The signed original deed papers safely on their way to the post office with the delivery boy, Rebecca sat back with a heavy thud in her padded office chair. In front of her lay a copy of the deed for her father's safekeeping.

"I have never signed anything quite so important." Talking aloud often produced a calming effect, but she doubted that tranquility would last long. The boy didn't know the envelope's contents or its importance, or that it required a signature of someone not in the house at the time, so she directed him to ask the local constable in Celina to find Robert Gilpin and send him home immediately, hoping Papa hadn't boarded a train yet. Though Papa might think something horrid happened to one of his family, his speedy return would soothe her guilty conscience.

A horse and buggy thundered up the shell drive about thirty minutes later. Rebecca looked out the window and let out a relieved breath when she saw her father jump from the buggy. Thankful that Colleen and Hannah were out of the house for the afternoon, she made her way to the door just as he threw it open.

"Problem, daughter? Is anyone hurt? Ill? Your mother?"

"No, Papa, it's not like that. We are fine. No one is ill or injured." She glanced around, making sure no one else stood within earshot. "All is well, but I had to let you know immediately about...well, about a rather large *forged* signature."

"Explain please."

"Not here, sir. Perhaps in the office behind closed doors might be best." Rebecca took several suggestive steps toward the room where the deed copy lay.

"You made a decision about something? Solved a problem?" He followed but slower, his breath still coming in fast order.

"Problem yes. I did make a decision and only hope it's not an illogical one. I would say this problem is solved, but only you and time will tell me."

Seeing her squirm satisfied Papa, she could tell. She would not toss a worry on him to solve. He raised her to take care of business. His chest puffed up even as they entered the office, and he closed the door.

"Papa?"

"Yes?"

"There is a matter of some grave importance."

"Really? And what is that?"

Rebecca had his curiosity. As long as his family was safe, nothing else would be as important, despite what she might think. However, Papa might change his mind after she told him about the signature on that deed. She clasped her hands in front of her while her gaze focused somewhere over his head.

"Mama received a letter while you were gone. Inside were pages to a deed, the one we knew you were waiting on. But, you see, you weren't here. Mama said you might be gone for several days, and the letter arrived late...far later than you expected. There was a matter of a signature and a speedy return in order for you to secure the deed, sir." She stopped speaking in order to form her thoughts correctly.

He waited for her to continue. "The paperwork is secured, correct?"

"Yes, sir, but I had to sign them." She gave an imperceptible nod, lifted her chin higher, and said, "I forged your signature, sir. I am accustomed to doing that often but not on such a critical document. I...pulled out a new pen and signed your name to it myself." Having gotten out the worst part, she talked quickly to get the rest out and over. "I sealed the envelope and returned it to the boy who brought it. He took it straight to the post. I asked him to return with a note from Postmaster King affirming that. I did not indicate you were away from home."

Rebecca thought she'd done the right thing. She wasn't sure if her father would agree. Though her audacity landed him the deed to a valuable property, thereby pleasing him immensely, not to say adding to his wealth, she worried that her action in this particular case might bring trouble. Signing for hotel and railway bills was one thing. Signing a deed to property was an entirely different matter.

Papa stood silent, his gaze on his daughter's face. Finally, he gave voice to his thoughts. "The deed was critical. I agree. The circumstances were extraordinary. While I do worry about that R. E. Gilpin being questioned in the future, that action in no way diminishes my pride in you, daughter... Rebecca. Your quick action saved the day. Your confession shows you to be a woman of honor." He walked forward and placed both hands on her shoulders, giving them a hard squeeze. "Your actions worked though I hope such dilemma never arises again. You were right to make sure the document arrived at the post office. I saw that the boy's reward was suitable for the performance of his duties. As for forging my signature on such an important document..." He let that hang for a moment, knowing the silence would have an impact on his eldest daughter. "I do not like that action, but in this one matter, it was necessary. Shan't happen again, I hope."

She felt the color slowly return to her face. "No, sir."

Rebecca wanted to take a deep breath, both because Papa wasn't furious with her and because she had stood in one place, under his inscrutable gaze, far too long. A sheen of perspiration wet her upper lip and forehead. She fervently wished she could pile her long hair on top of her head in a suitable style and allow the back of her neck to cool, she was that nervous.

"Now, my dear, if there is nothing else, I think we can adjourn to lunch. Mrs. Gordon promised to make a delightful dinner and serve it under the oaks for us all." He rounded the edge of the desk and tucked Rebecca's arm into the crook of his then walked her out the open French doors to the table beneath the trees. Just before they joined Mama and the other girls, he leaned over and whispered, "I'm not mad at you, darling, but whatever bright young man you marry might not be so amiable. Best to avoid possible jail time, my dear."

Beside him, Rebecca swallowed so hard she hurt. With her eyes on the ground, she softly murmured, "Yes, Papa."

———

How can he be so casual about me signing that deed? How can he then dismiss the entire affair and enjoy lunch and never turn a hair about the possibility of wrongdoing? Rebecca sat at the writing desk in her room. The open window before her admitted occasional breezes, fitful at best, still at worst.

Once again, she wondered about her father. His charm. His seemingly light touch when it came to interacting with people. He often treated his daughters as...she searched for a word that properly described her thoughts. Adornments. That was it. He returned from his many trips, expecting adoration from a waiting audience of loving admirers. He flitted among the girls, then sat with his wife, but never really had lengthy conversations with any of them. Only now was she seeing her father for what he was—a delightful man who required adulation to boost his self-esteem.

"I think nothing less of you, Papa," she whispered. "But I really wish you were a man I could admire as well as love." Sadly, her father was a charming rogue. "Perhaps that is a bit harsh," she admitted to the fly that settled on the screen just beyond where she sat, writing to a friend from the ladies' school she had attended.

Knowing her father better now than a day before, Rebecca pondered the relationship between Papa and Mama. True, her mother's health did not permit physical relations. Papa often visited Mama in her rooms, but their conversations remained light and frivolous. Inconsequential at best. At least while the girls were around.

Does Papa see Mama as a symbol rather than a person to love, cherish, and honor unto death?

Rebecca rubbed her forehead. "Too many questions today, fly." She waved a hand at the offending fly and shooed him away from the screen. Seeing the gardens in bloom and smelling the sweet scents of summer's mowed hayfields not far away, she sealed her letter and grabbed her bonnet.

"A walk will do me good."

Down the stairs she went and into the kitchen. "I'm walking to the post office, Mrs. Gordon."

"The girls should be home soon. Enjoy a quiet stroll." Mrs. Gordon never missed a beat of rolling out pastry for a game pie as she spoke.

"That I will. Thank you." With an apple in one hand, letters in her pocket, and bonnet strings tied loosely under her chin, Rebecca set off to refresh her spirits while taking a shortcut through the acres of their property.

Chapter 6
What a Foolish Girl!

Once again, Papa was going out of town. He would be gone two weeks, maybe a few days more. His itinerary said New York City, Philadelphia, and Chicago. Before his departure, he invited two bankers from Albany to join the family for dinner.

Hannah, of course, was too young to dine with company.

Colleen wasn't asked to join the party either. She protested being left out of the evening's activities. "I'm eighteen, Papa. I have just finished at Miss Marley's school. She says I'm a proper young lady now. I think I deserve to join the party tonight. I demand that I be allowed to attend."

Rebecca sat close by that afternoon and almost groaned aloud at her sister's mistake. If Colleen had *asked* to attend instead of demanding, Papa might have relented. She would hazard a guess that Papa wasn't sure he could control his middle daughter if she became willful. Rebecca could have told her father that Colleen would never embarrass the family. But the man never asked for her opinion on the subject.

"Not this time, my dear. Perhaps in the future you'll be allowed to join us." Papa walked away, the discussion closed. Rebecca saw the disappointment on his face, though Colleen did not.

Colleen met the gentlemen anyway though she didn't dine with them. Mama considered it good manners to at least introduce her younger daughters to their guests. She asked Papa to introduce them before sending them upstairs.

Hattie answered the door that evening and escorted Mr. Bolt and Mr. Adams into the drawing room where Robert waited.

Once again, Rebecca gave thanks that Mama wasn't the collecting kind of person as so many of her era were. Friends laid knickknacks over every flat surface in their homes, especially the drawing room. Rebecca often felt crowded amid what she considered clutter. Done for prestige, she was glad to see a lovely drawing room here with dark comfortable furniture, brightly polished cherry tables, fashionable pictures on the walls and a beautiful fireplace and mantel. The simplicity alone showed prestige without being ostentatious.

Mama and the girls entered before Papa offered the men brandy. He introduced his family with pride, his face alight with pleasure. Bolt and Adams took Mama's hand with care and kissed it. Each one nodded to the girls. Only Rebecca would remain with the adults. Colleen and Hannah answered several questions, then Mama dismissed them to return upstairs.

True to her nature, Hannah left quietly. Colleen, however, caught Rebecca's glance and stuck out her tongue. When Rebecca gasped, her sister grinned, at which both sisters broke into smiles. The give and take of sisterly affection passed quickly. Colleen had *demanded* to be part of the evening, and Papa had refused permission. She was self-confident enough, Rebecca knew, that the question would come up again. Perhaps her sister had learned her lesson that afternoon, though. Maybe next time she would *ask* instead of *demand*.

———

After Papa left, Hannah sulked. Though Mama enjoyed hearing her read, the stillness wore on the youngster. She often came away from her mother's rooms in a bit of a snit. The temper never lasted long, but Hannah had few friends to play with. The family lived too far out of town for her to walk there alone, and her sisters weren't always available to walk with her and wait while she played.

Colleen often sat by herself, sometimes reading or under the trees out in the garden, simply swinging. When Rebecca asked if things were all right with her, the girl gave her a bright smile and replied that beauty and wonder filled her days. Rebecca thought that a rather odd answer but seeing as this particular summer remained comfortable with mild days and only a few gentle showers, she assumed Colleen referred to her free time now that she'd left the finishing school.

With no one to talk to one afternoon, Rebecca headed to the shoreline of Grand Lake, as Hannah called it, having shortened the longer name. Peter Gordon would be working somewhere in the forest that ran along the border of their land, and he always spoke with her. If he worked in the gardens around the house, he often allowed her to help, much as Mama did in the past.

Nearer the water's edge, she wished she'd brought a

shawl. Her friend May Evans, who moved with her family to Atlanta, Georgia, often wrote how quickly the summer warmed and how walking became a task in the heat. Here the days were warming but still cool in the shade.

In the distance, she heard the sound of an axe. Mr. Gordon must be trimming some of the smaller trees. Rebecca tossed a few rocks in the lake, admiring the rings that spread in all directions. A small mallard landed and marred the beauty of the last rock ring. Ready to visit with her friend, she gathered her skirts and walked away from the shore into the edge of the property.

She ran up a knoll and stopped with the gardener's name on her lips only to be struck silent by the sight of a younger man wielding the ax. Mr. Gordon stood to one side, evidently giving advice on the best way to trim a yew tree.

"Now who the devil is that?" she murmured to a squirrel chattering on a branch nearby. A young man, wearing a soft-brim cap and rough jacket, worked beside Mr. Gordon. She could see he was taller than the gardener. She'd never seen this person before.

Leery of barging in on the two, she watched for a while unseen at the top of the small hill. The younger person finished trimming the tree and turned to another, the gardener showing him what to cut. When he was done, limbs lay scattered knee deep around them. Together, they stacked the limbs. Once, Rebecca thought the man might have spotted her, so she ducked behind a thick oak. *Silly to hide,* she chided herself, *but I've never seen him before.*

Before she could think of a good reason to step forward —though she had one when she went there to begin with— the two men shouldered their axes and headed away from the cleared area.

"Now, where are they off to?" She slid around the trunk and followed them, but not closely. Unless they veered off, she knew their general direction. Brush and a few thorns caught the hem of her skirt, so she gathered them as high as her knees and hoped her stockings would be intact after her adventure.

Mr. Gordon and his companion left the shelter of the trees and made their way to the garden where Colleen had been sitting fifteen minutes earlier. She was nowhere in sight now. Rebecca stopped and again hid behind a tree, her breath coming a bit fast after her trip through the forest.

Odd how a person sees a place but never really pays attention to it. She'd been born in that house and grown up there, leaving only long enough to attend finishing school. Even then, she'd come home each weekend and holiday. As Mr. Gordon showed off his prize blooms, she gazed over the garden as if seeing them like that young man...for the first time.

Her mother and grandmother had designed the garden after her parents bought the house. Her mother's parents were dead before Rebecca was born, but Mama always gave Grandmother Gilpin credit for creating a country garden like the one she remembered from her youth in England.

The garden faced Grand Lake then wrapped around both sides of the three-story house. A shell road dipped down off a shallow hill to run in front of the house then turned and ran along the lakeshore, twisting and passing other homes along the way. Abundant rose bushes graced the front of the house. A visitor would see phlox and Sweet William to one side of the house and more roses and brilliant orange-spotted Tiger Lilies on the shore side. But only invited friends viewed the magnificent gardens behind the Gilpin home.

From Rebecca's vantage point at the edge of the tree line, she saw the huge peony bushes with bees buzzing noisily around the huge, fragile, shell-colored blooms. Their fragrance filled the area on a warm summer day. Beyond those, nearest the house, stood tall larkspur with their multicolored blossoms. Nearer her hiding place, foxglove waved in the shore breeze, their tiny blooms looking like miniature bells clustered along the sturdy limbs. Each side of the horseshoe-shaped garden ended near the shore with abundant rose bushes in pink, white, and red.

While Mama loved each flower in her garden, she loved most the delicate roses that graced the front of the house and shoreline. When life bothered Rebecca, she worked beside Peter Gordon to take care of the flowers her mother loved but could no longer deal with.

Seeing Peter take up a white rose and show it to the other man, she remembered...

"Each color means something, you know," Mama told Rebecca. She reached over and touched a red bloom. "See, blood red means passion. A passion for living. I wish I were more like these," she whispered as she took her daughter's hand and led her to a vibrant pink rose. "Pink stands for happiness." She touched the little girl's chubby eight-year-old cheek with one slim finger.

"May's mama has yellow roses all over her yard."

"Dorthea Evens doesn't believe in the language of the flowers." Mama's mouth pinched tight, and her eyes squinted ever so slightly.

"What's that mean, Mama? Language? Flowers can't

talk." Rebecca moved away from the rose bush as if it might speak to her.

"No, dearest. Flower colors remind big people of things. Like happiness. Yellow is not a happy color."

"What's it mean?"

"Yellow is for infidelity." The woman must have realized what she said but wasn't willing to explain to a child, so she pulled her to a mound of white roses. "Now, these are the best."

Not sure she understood what her mother was saying, Rebecca whispered, "They're white."

"Indeed. And white is for purity," Felicity agreed.

"What's purity, Mama?"

Seeing the snowy white roses in the distance, Felicity smiled. "Purity means cleanliness, darling."

The young Rebecca held up her hands and asked in a little worried voice, "Do the roses know I didn't wash my hands before I ate?"

Felicity held her smile; Rebecca could tell she wanted to laugh. But a wise mother tries not to hurt her children's feelings. "No, dear. The roses don't care about your grubby hands. However..." She winked at her daughter and nodded to the less than clean hands. "I do. Now it's time to wash those hands, or Mrs. Gordon won't let you eat. Papa won't let you sit at the table."

"Really, Mama?" Rebecca asked in wonder.

"Well, maybe..."

The memories faded fast as the gardener and garden boy came into view from the far side of the house. A boy—Rebecca refused to call him a man. What *man* would be sneaking around her family's home, cozying up to the hired help? Though to be honest, she never thought of Peter or Charlotte Gordon as hired help. This boy was talking to her friend. Taking the old man's time away from his tasks. One of which was caring for the garden.

Did the older man value this boy's conversation more than hers? That boy was in *her* garden. An instant flare of jealousy hit Rebecca. She worked there with Mr. Gordon when she needed to think. The reason she went searching for the gardener in the first place returned to Rebecca. Her concern for Hannah and Colleen. Now she had two concerns...her sisters and this newcomer. This intruder in her safe world.

Never one to foist responsibility off onto another, she gathered her skirts once more and stomped out of the tree coverage, past the peony bushes to accost this...this garden boy.

Her temper rose with each step. This male was trying to usurp her place in Mr. Gordon's good will.

In a clipped, frigid tone, she demanded, "And who might you be, garden boy?"

Mr. Gordon stepped forward, ready to introduce the young man with him. But the boy—young man—stepped forward first. He pulled the bill of his cap and dipped his head. "Thomas Willey."

"Who gave you permission to wander through my property?" Rebecca corrected her question. "Our property."

"Mr. Gordon knows more about plants than anyone I've ever met. Friends told me about him. I want to learn how to grow things like he does."

"Oh." His words stole some of the wind out of her puffed-up sails.

"I'd like permission to continue working with him, if that's all right."

"Oh." She realized how silly she sounded when that second *oh* came out. "I suppose..." She slipped her hands off her hips and clasped them in front of her, though her chin remained in the air. "I suppose that will be all right. Mind you, don't take any plants or seeds. My mother and Mr. Gordon have worked especially hard to gather these. And you can only stay if Mr. Gordon says you may."

Peter Gordon nodded to show the other's presence didn't bother him.

Once again, the boy touched the bill of his cap. "Thank you."

Rebecca could have sworn Mr. Gordon smiled, but his hand covered a cough about that time.

"If the family comes out into the garden, you are not to be here. Go work somewhere in the forest." She waved her hand, shooing him off like a fly.

"I can do that."

For a few seconds, Rebecca and the young man stared at each other. He was thicker than she first realized, not fat but more muscled. But then swinging an ax could build muscles, she supposed. Brown hair peeked out from the front edge of his cap, falling in a small wave over his forehead. His hands were big while his large brown eyes faced her square on.

A blush rose up her neck to her face, heating her skin to the point she blinked and took a step back.

"Be sure you do, garden boy."

The only way she could leave the fellow's presence was to nod and turn on her heel, so that's what she did. As she walked to the back porch, she felt the young man's eyes on her back. Realizing she walked faster, she intentionally slowed to a more decorous walk. Just before she closed the door to the back hallway, however, she grabbed the end of her braid and twisted it as she peeked out to see that the young man had not turned away. He stood as she last saw him, though Mr. Gordon shook his head.

Why is he shaking his head? Why haven't they returned to work? she wondered. *He has freckles.* That thought made her smile.

Chapter 7
Distasteful Relatives

Rebecca entered her mother's suite of rooms to discover the furniture covered with colorful cloth. "What's this?" Several boxes rattled, and two women stood up on the far side of the room. "Mama?"

"Come, darling, and meet Jenny and Theresa Clark. They make the most divine gowns. Your father has given permission for them to create some lovely gowns for you. They will be ready around the first of July."

Across the room, the women—both twig-thin— dipped a courtesy. Rebecca nodded as she moved to her mother's side. "Are these the women who make your gowns?"

Her mother seldom left the house, not even to attend church. Papa often took her for a carriage ride at dusk, sometimes when few were out to see her. Mama received new gowns these days by special delivery, apparently from the shop run by these two women.

Rebecca started to sit, but material lay draped everywhere.

"Jenny and Theresa have made my gowns for years. Now

they've come to measure you and see what colors will suit your complexion."

Hannah sat quietly on the stool on the other side of their mother. "Does this mean Rebecca is grown up? Will she get married and leave?" Her pale green eyes peered out of her childishly chubby face, worry pulling her forehead into a frown.

"Would that bother you, dearest?" Mama leaned over and kissed her child's forehead, then smoothed the worry lines out with a thin finger.

"I don't like it when someone goes away."

"Papa goes away all the time." Mama pushed the light-colored hair off Hannah's forehead.

"But he always comes home. Henry didn't." Hannah slapped a hand across her mouth, while her eyes grew large as saucers. "I'm sorry." She turned teary eyes to Rebecca.

Count on Hannah to see things we want to ignore. Like Henry's loss. Rebecca never realized how the man's death affected her sister. She vowed to be more aware of Hannah's feelings when things happened in the family.

Rebecca scooped up her sister and hugged her. "I know you didn't mean to say that, Hannah. We all miss Henry. But God wanted him, so He took him." She wiped tears off her sister's face and turned to sit on the stool where the little girl had been sitting. "Now, my birthday is coming up soon—"

"August first!"

"Correct, and you must help me pick out some patterns and fabric for new gowns for me to wear when I turn twenty-one, and I gain my inheritance from Grandmother Gilpin."

Even as the dressmakers, Hannah, and Mama discussed gowns, Rebecca wondered if she was worthy of being someone's wife. Or had her fiancé's death been a sign, saying it best to remain unmarried?

Papa told her once that he mourned the loss of young Henry. Henry recognized the worth of a woman and would have made a grand partner for his oldest daughter, he'd said. After Henry's death though, Papa reminded her that other men would come calling on her once July fourth passed.

New gowns...would that make her feel new? An image of that young man she'd met in the garden eased into her mind. What would he think if he saw her in a new dress? She wondered what sort of husband he'd make.

Rebecca groaned, but not too loudly, or Mama might think she did not favor the lovely spring green sprigged material in her hand. Men. Husbands. Gowns. Logical answers to questions lay out there somewhere...she simply did not want to think about such things as men and husbands at the moment. Today she would step forward, making progress into a brighter world by way of beautiful gowns.

———

Papa returned from his extended trip several hours after Rebecca's new dresses—subtle in coloring—arrived. The girls fell on him, smothering him with hugs and kisses. Rags tried jumping on Papa until the man took to one knee and hugged the dog as well as ruffling his long fur before sending the dog back to Mr. Gordon. When peace settled, he hung his hat on the newel post and led the way to Mama's rooms.

To Rebecca's surprise, Mama mentioned the gowns and asked Rebecca to bring them so Papa could see them. Colleen helped carry one, while Rebecca carried the other. Hannah carried matching shoes for each dress.

"What is Mama planning, having you bring in your dresses?" Colleen carefully held the pale pink dress with tiny gray flowers so it did not drag on the floor.

"I have no idea. The Fourth isn't for another month." Rebecca hurried to take the lead.

"You two worry about things you cannot control."

Rebecca and Colleen almost collided as they stopped and faced Hannah, their mouths gaping open. The younger sister stood with shoes in both hands and hands propped on her hips. She should have looked a bit silly, but for some reason she appeared quite mature. Her comment definitely gave the older girls something to think about.

"Young miss, when did you become so wise?" Rebecca bent over the dress she held and kissed the top of Hannah's head.

"I have several wise people to listen to in this house," Hannah replied as she eased past Rebecca.

Colleen winked at Hannah as she took the lead to Mama's door. "I bet you haven't picked up a lot of wisdom from me."

"You might be surprised, Colleen." With that enigmatic statement, Hannah tucked one set of shoes under her arm, turned the doorknob, gathered up the shoes again, and used a hip to push the door open. "You would be surprised, sister," she repeated as she disappeared into her mother's shadowy rooms.

Colleen and Rebecca lifted shoulders in a *what was that about* shrug. They carried the dresses into their mother's room and waited to see what Mama would do with them.

Papa sat like a king in his armchair next to Mama as Rebecca held the dresses up against herself. He liked both the pale pink one as well as the soft spring green one that she especially liked.

"Now, Robert, I want your approval, so that Rebecca can enter the summer wearing something more lively than the soft mourning colors she has worn since last year. So many people..." Rebecca knew she meant men. "...will be out riding and visiting friends, and she might meet someone she fancies."

Rebecca knew better than to roll her eyes. Her father would take exception to the rudeness, especially if it hurt her mother's feelings. She sighed instead but covered it by rearranging the dress.

Papa sat in silence for several seconds, the ladies around him young and old holding their breath. Wearing the dresses a full month before the mourning year ended could be cause for raised brows in the neighborhood. "Henry asked you to marry him," he said finally. "You two never had a chance to actually marry. Wearing those somber dresses was a way of honoring his memory. However, I agree with your mother on this issue. You did him honor in your dress and manner for months now. I believe he would approve of you going out again."

Rather than run to him, hug him like a mad woman then sashay out the door, Rebecca slipped over to her mother first. "Thank you, Mama." She spoke softly as she placed a kiss on paper-thin cheeks.

She did the same for her father, a kiss and quiet words, thanking him for his leniency and generosity.

Once the door closed on the three girls, they stood in dumb silence for all of three seconds before breaking into smiles and suppressed giggles.

"Race you!" Rebecca hugged the dress to her bosom and ran down the hall.

"Hey, wait for us!" Her sisters slid into her room, closed the door, and watched Rebecca spend an hour trying on her new gowns.

———

Mama made an announcement over dinner the next night. "Uncle Eugene and Cousin Ross are coming to visit."

"Oh, I'm sorry, dearest. I am taking the early train to Chicago tomorrow morning." Papa sipped his water and dabbed his lips afterwards. He did not look especially upset at not seeing his brother-in-law and nephew.

"You can't delay your leaving until after they leave, Robert?" Mama laid a hand on her chest as her eyes grew wide. She even sounded a bit...desperate.

That's an odd reaction to Papa leaving. Maybe Mama doesn't want to meet her brother and nephew without him by her side, Rebecca thought. "May I join you in the parlor tomorrow, Mama? We can visit...the four of us." The offer was a generous one for Rebecca to make, seeing as she didn't care for either her uncle or cousin.

"May I come as well, Mama?" Colleen appeared less than eager though she asked sincerely.

"Oh, would you, dears? That's so lovely of you." Mama's hand relaxed back to her fork. She actually ate a few bits of her meal.

"Yes, Mama." Colleen turned her attention to her meal but ate far more vigorously than her mother did.

"Certainly, Mama." Again, Mama's problem. Rebecca's solution. Logical or not, she hoped she would not regret spending time with these particular relatives. Come to think on it, they were the only ones that her family had left.

———

"I may never think of the parlor with such love after seeing our uncle and cousin in there so often. All that hominess is wonderful. Soft green walls. Deep striped sofas and floral chairs, a cozy fireplace, windows that allow sun and the breezes in. That room ought to be just for the family. And I don't mean Uncle and Cousin."

"I agree," Colleen said as she climbed into bed that night, "but it's not up to us. Sooner or later, we can banish him though," she added with a fiery sword-swishing gesture which made Rebecca laugh.

———

Uncle Eugene Callaway and his son Ross came to visit at least once a month. They traveled by covered buggy. Eugene and Ross worked together in business in Dayton, but Rebecca did not know exactly what that business was. Nor did she care. Uncle Eugene reminded Rebecca of a snake, handsome but dangerous, with his fancy clothing, puffed-up chest and long beard. That was the first impression she had of him when she was old enough to understand that the man could visit anytime he wanted...with Mama or Papa's permission, of course. Her cousin Ross resembled a penny dreadful villain. Slick when talking to those he meant to impress, but ruthless when things did not go his way. Though Ross was a hand-some man with his soft brown hair, parted carefully to one side and a thin mustache below soft gray eyes, his attitude toward his cousins was not handsome or soft. He showed that side of himself only to the girls, but never to his Aunt Felicity or Uncle Robert Gilpin.

Not that either Callaway male ever did anything to distress Mama. Or Hannah or Colleen. However, the last time Ross visited, he stood too close to Rebecca and whispered in her ear, close enough to ruffle the hair at the side of her head.

"The last thing I want to do is sit in a room with Ross and Uncle Eugene," Rebecca whispered to Colleen as they left the table. "But I didn't want to see Mama in distress, thinking she would talk to them alone."

"Uncle is slimy," Colleen said, getting directly to the point.

"That's an awful thing to say," Rebecca said as she shooed Hannah into the parlor, "but I'm afraid that's how I see him as well."

"Ross is as well. Have you noticed that Uncle likes to have the last word in a conversation?" Colleen settled on the long sofa and pulled a soft throw over her legs.

"I hadn't really noticed. I tend to woolgather when he comes." Rebecca picked up the book she'd been reading to the girls. "But I will listen more carefully tomorrow."

Chapter 8
A Massive Problem to Solve

"Dear Sister, how are you?"

"Well enough, Eugene." Felicity allowed her brother to take her hand and kiss the knuckles.

Rebecca refused to roll her eyes in disgust, but the feeling almost choked her. Colleen stood beside her and started to give a derogatory snort, but Rebecca managed to grab her arm and squeeze hard enough to stifle the sound.

However, Cousin Ross saw the gesture and interpreted it correctly. His eyes squinted slightly, and he shifted position so that he could watch both girls more carefully.

"And Ross, you are well?" Felicity stood, though one hand rested for support against the back of a sofa. As her nephew answered, she took a seat before the tea table and nodded to Hattie, the maid, who entered and set a tray down in front of her.

"As you say, Aunt Felicity, well enough." Ross turned his sharp gaze back to the girls. "Ladies, you're looking quite lovely for a warm summer day." His eyes almost devoured Rebecca. "I'm glad to see you in brighter colors these days, Becca. Those mourning clothes did you no justice."

Every word from her cousin sounded condescending. How Colleen held her tongue was a mystery—and a miracle —as far as Rebecca was concerned. For once, she thanked her mother for making her wear her hair long. Not in a braid today. She wore it loose but down, like a proper young woman...not a lady yet.

While Mama and Eugene apparently had grown up in an amicable home, he and his son seemed to have a burning desire to dominate. Uncle Eugene was not like the man Mama portrayed in her stories about them as youngsters.

The man learned to be sharp and devious in business, Rebecca assumed. Or perhaps his true nature emerged after he left home and his parents died.

Ross cleared his throat, his attention still on the girls.

He expects some reply. Rebecca groaned, but only to herself. "My fiancé deserved to be mourned properly, Cousin Ross. I did so in his honor." She threw a quick glance at her uncle, checking to make sure he paid no attention to their conversation. He sat talking to Mama. Rebecca added in a quieter voice to Ross. "Honor—something I believe you are unfamiliar with, sir."

Ross bristled but remained quiet, though his face turned almost purple in anger. Anything he could say would make him look like the cur he was. At one time, he was engaged to a lovely girl from upstate, but when her family lost their fortune and the woman came down with consumption, he disengaged himself and never bothered to speak to her or her family again. Though few knew the exact details of the broken relationship, thinking the woman called off the engagement after becoming ill, Eugene gave his sister a more accurate picture of what really happened. Mama passed those details on to Rebecca, who in turn passed them on to Colleen.

The girls feared that Ross' attention might turn to them, seeing as the Gilpin fortune was steady. But Mama never mentioned anything. So while they did not exactly rest easy, the two never forgot that they were of marriageable age. Not only that, but Rebecca would inherit a fortune if Papa and Mama died, or she reached her next birthday.

That thought rested uneasily with Rebecca. She would discuss it with Colleen later, but for the moment, the girls, Mama, Uncle Eugene, and Cousin Ross enjoyed afternoon tea.

"You know, Felicity, Rebecca will be twenty-one soon. She is almost on the shelf, as they say, when it comes to marrying." Uncle Eugene poured milk in his tea, turning it almost white. He spoke so innocently, as a girl might speak about another.

Her uncle completely ignored the fact that the person he talked about sat not six feet away and was neither deaf nor blind. Nor stupid.

"Rebecca is the rock of our family, Eugene. Henry's death devastated us. He would have made such a wonderful addition to our family. He was level-headed and knew the worth of our darling daughter." Mama sipped her tea and sounded just as innocent, completely ignoring Eugene's insulting hint. The conversation played like cat and mouse between the adults, while the children sat, teacups in hand, wondering who would win this war of words.

For war, it was. Papa would grow incensed when Mama mentioned her brother. He would curl his lip and pace as he recounted Eugene's attempts to bring Rebecca into *his* family. Ross seemed as eager to marry her as Eugene was to gain the fortune she would inherit. Rebecca often thought that if Eugene could hasten Papa and Mama's deaths, he would. The Callaway's attempts to ingratiate themselves into the Gilpin family had failed so far. That might not always be the case.

According to the inheritance agreement Papa set up for Rebecca, she *would* indeed inherit on her twenty-first birthday. She would be a free woman at that point to choose whom she would marry. Until such time, Rebecca's eligibility as a bride rested in the hands of her father. Papa made it clear several years earlier what he thought of Eugene Callaway and his son's attempts to woo his eldest daughter.

So on this warm early summer afternoon, tension flowed under the surface as Ross shot hot glances Rebecca's way that made her uncomfortable. Colleen squirmed in anger, while brother and sister bandied words, neither gaining ground toward Eugene's ultimate goal.

The problem was that Ross needed to accomplish that seemingly impossible task before Rebecca's birthday. All three cousins were aware of that timeline.

———

"Did I not say Cousin Ross is slimy?" Colleen never minced words when the three girls were together, though she saved her more horrid words for when Hannah was not around.

"Slimy? Like a frog? Or a worm?" Hannah knelt in the window seat of Rebecca's room, her nose resting against the screen. She never took her gaze off whatever had caught her attention outside, but she listened to what the girls said.

"I suppose you could say that, sister." Colleen joined

Hannah on the seat but sat looking back into the room, her elbows back, resting on the windowsill.

"Cousin Ross is too full of himself if you ask me," the youngest commented. Those words no sooner out of her mouth, she spotted something. "May I go outside now, Rebecca? Uncle Eugene and Cousin Ross are gone. They're not interested in me, anyway."

"Too true." Colleen spoke in an undertone that Rebecca heard, but Hannah did not.

"Yes, darling, but what is out there that is so very interesting?" Rebecca moved to the window and studied the yard. All she saw was Mr. Gordon...and garden boy.

What is his name? She'd forgotten the minute she left his presence, though she had not forgotten how he looked.

"Mr. Gordon is teaching Thomas about the flowers and trees in our garden. Thomas wants to go to college and learn about ag..." Hannah seemed to lose the word for which she searched. "Agr..."

"Agriculture, dear?" Rebecca watched as the gardener and his follower mulched roses.

"That's the word. Thomas is keen on planting and keeping those plants alive. May I go?"

"Certainly, but don't bother them as they work, and don't get dirty. Mama will fuss if you come to dinner looking like a mud bug."

"Thank you, Rebecca." Hannah flew out the door, the sound of her boots thudding down the back staircase.

"That girl knows no fear and makes friends too easily." Colleen turned to watch her sister's progress across the yard. While she stood several feet from Mr. Gordon, she had apparently made friends with the garden boy so stood nearer him, peppering him with questions, it seemed.

"At least she doesn't have to worry about a man wanting to marry her. Not for several years yet, anyway." Rebecca sat beside Colleen, and both turned their backs to the window.

"Is it wrong that Papa has given the bulk of the family fortune to me, Colleen?"

"He made provisions for me and Hannah. You're in charge of seeing to that, eventually. Papa trusts you. So does Mama. *I* trust you." Colleen was not a person who touched others without reason, so when she reached over and laid a hand on Rebecca's arm, Rebecca slipped a hand over it in gratitude.

"I doubt few girls would ever say that about older sisters. Thank you. I fear though—"

"—that Ross is looking to catch you and very soon?" Colleen finished.

"Yes," Rebecca replied. "I fear that Uncle will talk Mama into an arrangement. Mama only wants my happiness but doesn't see how much I loathe Ross. If Uncle Eugene gets his way, Papa's plans for my independence will be fairly null and void. According to Papa, that would be like tearing up a contract."

"Count on Papa to put such matters in terms of business. But Becca, aren't you scared?"

"To be honest, I'd like to disappear until my birthday. Mama doesn't seem to understand the implications of such an engagement. She knows that I gain money when I reach twenty-one. She doesn't think clearly about this, I fear. Now that my year of mourning has ended, she will bring me out on the marriage market." Rebecca moved from the window to a chair. Throwing herself in the comfort of the seat in an unladylike fashion, she mused in silence. For once, Colleen remained quiet.

"When I marry, I want to marry for love. Not status or fortune. I'm not such a snob that any man will do. If I marry at age thirty, then so be it, as long as it is *my* choice. Does that sound selfish?"

"I don't think so," Colleen replied, "but then I am the middle daughter, neither the darling youngest nor the reliable oldest. I am allowed to become myself, while you must conform, in some ways at least. Marrying for love doesn't sound so bad to me, though."

"You have a rather cynical attitude toward your position in the family, sister." Rebecca came back to her younger sister and stood over her. "You are loved and safe. There are many out in the world who cannot say the same. Whatever decisions you make should be logical, made for the right reasons. But if they turn out to not be so logical and with consequences then as Papa says—"

"That would be a problem, and I must solve it," Colleen finished. "I will make those kinds of decisions, I'm sure. I'm allowed, as I said. No one particularly cares what I do. But if there are consequences..." Colleen shrugged and stood, brushing the wrinkles out of her cotton skirt. "I shall deal with it."

"But not alone, dear. Remember, you have family, and we love you. No one wants to see you suffer, much less suffer alone."

"I know, Rebecca. I'll remember."

———

Papa returned home at midnight, almost three weeks after he left. That was the longest he had ever been gone from home. Rebecca happened to be up with Hannah who had overindulged in cake that evening and suffered a stomachache.

"Papa?" She had seen the buggy as it passed the house to the stable around back. Mr. Gordon would be fast asleep in the cottage. Papa would never ask the man to rise from his bed and take care of the horse when he could do it just as easily.

"It's me, Rebecca." Papa came through the back door into the kitchen, letting his suitcase thump to the floor. His face showed signs of fatigue, as if he had gone many hours without sleep.

Rebecca rushed to hug his neck. "You look worn out, Papa. Can I fix you a plate? You must be hungry." She moved to the icebox, but her father stopped her.

"Not now, dearest. I am indeed tired. Many things wear on my mind right now. They're worrisome, but not fearful."

He said that so she'd not worry. In the morning, he would explain his odd remark, she knew.

"If you're sure, sir."

"Yes. Go on up to bed..." His head snapped up, and he glanced around the room, suddenly aware his daughter was up in the middle of the night. "Is everything all right? You are up very late. Or is it very early?"

"Nothing is amiss but a tummy ache, Papa," Rebecca assured him. "Hannah ate too many sweets this evening, despite Mama's warning that she would suffer. I sat with her after she was sick. She is sleeping peacefully now. I'm going to bed if you don't need anything."

"No, darling. Get your rest." He tugged her nighttime braid just as he did when she was Hannah's age. "I'll surprise everyone at breakfast by making a grand entrance. Come, give your ol' father a kiss, then find your bed."

She not only kissed his cheek, but also hugged him extra tight. Papa had something on his mind, and she doubted he would rest easy despite how tired he appeared.

As she left the room, she glanced back. Papa sat at the small kitchen table with snatches of moonlight coming through the window. A fierce storm was coming, with boiling clouds and plenty of thunder and lightning. Papa had beaten the storm, but he looked so lost, sitting there. The scene struck her as ominous, though she had no idea why.

———

What is that? Rebecca's head came up from the pillow. She had just laid down, settling the sheet over her when she heard what sounded like a thud. Sitting up, she indulged in a moment of fear. Not willing to traipse through the house alone, she slipped on her soft night shoes and dressing gown and eased her door open. She should get her father, but as worn out as he looked earlier, he was probably sleeping heavily.

Rain had settled in after she left her father in the kitchen, so the storm was all she could hear now. She slipped along the hall to Colleen's door. She entered and moved to the bed. Putting a hand over Colleen's mouth, she awakened her.

"I heard something in the house." Lightning flashed, and a tremendous clap of thunder accompanied a furious downpour.

"You mean you actually heard something over all that noise?" Colleen mumbled. More thunder followed lightning. The storm seemed to have settled in hard and fast.

"Yes, a thud. Somewhere near my door. Come on."

"Wish Papa was here." Colleen grumbled, though she

slipped on her own shoes and dressing gown.

"He is. I passed through the kitchen to return a dirty dish after sitting with Hannah. Papa walked in the back door. I'm not sure who was more surprised, him or me." Rebecca motioned Colleen to her side and opened the door. "He seemed worried about something." She spoke in such a low whisper that Colleen had to lean closer to hear.

"Go on. Let's see what has gotten us both up in the middle of the night." Colleen pushed Rebecca forward with a hand on her back.

The girls moved like ghosts down the hall, passed Mama's and Hannah's rooms. Together they looked over the upstairs railing. Seeing nothing in the foyer below, they crept down the staircase and checked out each room.

"Nothing." Rebecca stood in total darkness, her forehead wrinkled in a frown. "But I heard something...a heavy thud."

"Maybe it was Mama or Hannah, falling out of bed," suggested Colleen.

"Oh Lord, I never thought of that!"

Rebecca lifted her nightclothes and ran up the stairs, her and Colleen practically colliding as they rounded the top of the stairs into the long hallway.

Quick as possible, each took a door, Rebecca her mother's and Colleen Hannah's. Seeing both in bed and asleep, they joined up again by a hall table.

"That only leaves Papa's room. But surely, he's sound asleep." She grabbed Colleen's hand and motioned down the hall. At Colleen's nod, they moved to Papa's door.

Easing the door open, unsure what to tell their father if he woke and found them in his room, they left the door open but moved cautiously into the room. Rebecca neared the far side of the bed, but her foot hit something.

"I don't think Papa's in bed." Colleen had approached the bed from the other side and had a better view of the covers.

"I bumped into something. Quick, Colleen, light the gas, and let's see what is happening here."

A spark and pop and the gas jet caught, lighting the room in a soft yellow glow.

Rebecca slapped a hand over her mouth to restrain a scream that lingered just inside her lips.

"Papa?" The form she'd hit was Papa, sprawled face down on the floor at the side of his bed, his dressing gown open, flared out around him. She dropped to her knees and shook his shoulder. "Papa?"

Colleen dropped down beside her and felt his wrist. "I read about this in a book," Colleen said. "You can feel a person's heartbeat here." She raised a stricken face to her sister. "No heartbeat. Maybe I did it wrong. Let me try somewhere else." She reached under Papa's head and laid a finger alongside his neck. "Nothing. Rebecca, I can't find a pulse!"

"Help me turn him over." Rebecca slid her hand under her father's face and placed a hand on his shoulder. Colleen helped, and together they rolled him onto his back.

Both girls fell back, their eyes wide in horror, hands to their mouths, holding back screams of terror. Before them lay a dead man, his eyes open, the glaze of death beginning to skim the surface, his jaw dropped too far and his tongue hanging out like a panting dog.

Dead. Robert Gilpin lay dead in the early morning hours with a furious storm hammering the house. Life had just presented two of the Gilpin girls a horrifying problem, and at the moment, they were incapable of finding a solution.

Chapter 9
An Unbelievable Plan

"Papa?" Colleen whispered, her body shaking, her knuckles buried deep in her mouth. Tears began rolling down her cheek. "Rebecca, is he...is he really...?"

A nod was all Colleen got. Rebecca sat in shock, too paralyzed with fear to speak. "This can't be. I just talked to him." She rocked back and forth, repeating, "I just talked to him."

"Rebecca, what do we do? Mama? Hannah?" Colleen sat immobile.

"Mama? Oh, Lord! What can we tell her?" Rebecca stopped rocking and lifted first one arm, then the other to wipe her face. "We can't tell her."

"What do you mean, we can't tell her?" Colleen instantly became angry. Her voice rose in near hysteria. "Our father—her husband—just died on his bedroom floor!"

A hand clamped over the girl's mouth, and Rebecca's other hand shook Colleen's shoulder so hard her head rocked back. "Quiet!"

"What do you mean, we can't—"

"Think about it, Colleen. Papa wasn't even coming home for two more days. Mama's not in the best health. How is she going to take this if we just bust into her room and announce that first, he's home, and second, oh by the way, he died less than an hour after he walked in?"

Colleen still shook but averted her eyes from the corpse in front of her. Jumping to her feet, she snatched the coverlet off her father's bed and pulled it over him. "I'm sorry, but I can't look at him like that. I don't want to remember him like that."

Rebecca stood and helped pull the cover straight, so it looked like a bump in the floor. A rather large, still bump. She ran a hand through her hair and ran both hands down her face. One hand came to rest across her mouth, her eyes far off, her mind running full tilt.

"A problem that needs a solution," Colleen mouthed as she stepped back.

"What is the problem, and maybe we can think of a solution?" A small voice interrupted the older girls' grief.

"Hannah Beatrice Gilpin! You scared the wits out of me!" Colleen fussed at her sister then shot a glance at Rebecca.

"Sister, you need to be in bed. Now!" Rebecca moved toward Hannah, praying the little girl saw and heard nothing more than they had a problem and needed an answer.

Meanwhile, the storm outside intensified, ramping up to match the tense atmosphere in the room.

"No, you have a problem. The Gilpin girls can always find a solution." Hannah stood like a boulder at the door to her father's room. "Tell me. I want to help."

"Dearest, we cannot," Rebecca said sadly.

"Why not?"

"Because..." Rebecca ran out of words. How does one tell a child that her father lies dead on the floor not ten feet away? *Thankfully, we covered the body.* She swallowed bile that threatened to rise when she realized she referred to Papa as *the body*.

"Something's happened, and you don't want me to know."

Hannah, normally the most docile child, took a stance like a mule, prepared to remain in the doorway until she got some answers.

"We can't, dearest," said Colleen, moving to stand beside Rebecca, their bodies blocking the corpse under the bed cover on the floor. "You won't understand, and it will make you unhappy. If you are unhappy, then Mama will want to know why. And when she finds out, then she will be unhappy." Colleen held her hands out to her side, palms up. "We have to figure out how to deal with this problem, but we don't want you involved."

"Truth?"

Colleen laid a hand on her sister's shoulder and squeezed gently. "Plain hard truth, Hannah."

Hannah stood in the doorway, her face turning from one sister to the other. Then she scanned the room, the part she could see.

"I saw, you know." Hannah let tears slide slowly down her cheeks. "Papa came home and..." In the past, she might have flung herself into Rebecca's arms in a fit of crying, but not this time. "Papa went to Heaven, didn't he? He wasn't coming home until Wednesday, but he came home early..." Hannah paused, sucking in a deep breath. "He came home where he is loved and safe and...died. Like my cat Marmalade."

Colleen looked at Rebecca, then Hannah. "Hannah has always amazed me at how perceptive she is. How grown-up she can be at times."

"The hard truth, as I put it, is just that, dearest," Rebecca said. "But we don't want you involved because...well, it's just not something a child should have to be involved in." Rebecca smoothed the hair off her sister's forehead, then brushed away a few remaining tears.

"May I see him?"

"I think it's best if you remember Papa like he was last time he was home." Colleen stuffed her hands in the pockets of her dressing gown, dropped her eyes, and shuffled her feet. "I will. Not like this," she said with a short nod toward the bedroom.

Hannah seemed reluctant to go. "Maybe...Maybe we should bury him and not tell anyone. Well, sooner or later, we'll have to tell Mama, but she might..." Hannah swallowed big enough that her sisters saw. Hannah dropped her voice and whispered, "Mama might die, too."

"Golly." Colleen always had a knack for voicing the situation as she saw it.

"There is a problem with this idea, though." Rebecca still stood rooted across Hannah's line of sight. "Papa's death will bring that problem running faster than a dog if he knows."

Colleen gasped. "Uncle Eugene!"

Hannah caught on fast. "Cousin Ross!"

"You know what Uncle will do, don't you?" Rebecca turned worried eyes to her sisters. "He will tell Mama that he and Ross need to move in with us, to *protect* and *guide* us. He has said as much before because Papa traveled so much."

"Are you joking?"

Rebecca could see red rising through Colleen. Her sister got mad easily and often held on to that temper for a long time.

"I am not joking. If he knows and suggests that he will maneuver Mama into allowing them the house. Once they are here, Ross will pursue me endlessly. He and Uncle will contrive to get me married before my birthday."

Colleen gasped again. "And what about Hannah and me?"

Rebecca sighed and laid a hand on each shoulder. "I am only guessing, but I suspect that while Ross pursues me, Uncle will use Mama's failing health to send Hannah to boarding school and you to some governess job as far from here as possible."

"Golly!"

Hannah burst into tears.

"Come here, Hannah." Rebecca gathered the little girl in her arms. Seeing Colleen standing so near with such a shocked expression, she gathered her in as well.

"So we have to keep...this...a...secret." Hannah hiccupped within the safety of her sisters' arms.

Rebecca shrugged her shoulders. "The last thing I want is Uncle Eugene and Cousin Ross around, and that will happen. I can almost guarantee it."

"So maybe we better do what I said...we bury Papa and keep it a secret...for as long as we can. At least until your birthday, Rebecca."

"But...but..."

"Becca, that may be our only chance to survive long enough for you to gain your inheritance and independence. And keep our family together." Colleen stood back, a strange look on her face, as if she could not believe she said such a thing.

"I can't even believe I am planning to go along with this idea." Rebecca started to pace like she sometimes did when thinking but caught herself the minute she glanced over her shoulder and saw the bedcover and the rather large bump.

"We need help." Hannah fisted one hand and thumped it into the palm of the other.

"Good Lord, the child is a miniature picture of Papa when she does that," Colleen observed.

"She's right, you know. We can't just toss Papa into a grave and get on as if nothing happened. Sooner or later, someone will come looking for him."

Both middle and younger sister stopped talking, giving the older sister time to think.

"When Mr. Gordon's father died, they called the doctor," Hannah offered, a frown settled between her brows, her eyes sad but her expression determined.

"Yes, of course. That's it. Doctor Vincent can come, see Papa, and write one of those papers like Mr. Gordon got. The paper says the man is dead and when it happened. That way, we at least have a witness. What do you think?" Rebecca forgot that Hannah should be in bed. It was all or nothing now. Gilpin problem. Gilpin girls' solution.

"Remember when you told Hannah about making logical decisions and hoping they don't turn out to be illogi-cal, like very bad for our future?" Colleen took hold of Rebecca's arm to get her attention, as the older girl seemed lost in thought again.

"Yes."

"If we call the doctor and he writes one of those papers

then goes home, that leaves us with the original problem. And there's only one solution I can think of."

"Go on, Colleen. You must have an answer to whatever you're thinking."

"After Doctor Vincent leaves—with no questions asked —we get Mr. Gordon to help move Papa and bury him...oh, out on the property somewhere. In a place we don't go."

"First the doctor and now Mr. Gordon." Rebecca turned a shrewd glance to Colleen. "You know, of course, that what Mr. Gordon knows, Mrs. Gordon will know."

"We need Mrs. Gordon, sister," said Hannah.

"We do? What do you mean?"

"We can't go to Mr. Gordon's house and leave Mama alone." Hannah shivered slightly. "I don't want to be alone with just Mama sleeping."

"I hadn't thought of that," Rebecca admitted.

"I will stay. But you must hurry." Colleen lifted her chin but drew one hand over her waist as if protecting herself. "I will not wait in here. I'll...I'll sit in the hallway. But hurry." She repeated that with just a touch of panic in her voice.

"Hannah, stay with Colleen."

"No."

"Please, sister."

"No. I am going with you."

With two sisters turned stubborn mules, Rebecca had no choice. "All right. Colleen guards the room from the hall. Hannah and I will get our boot, capes, and hats and run to Mr. Gordon's house. Thank God it's not that far away."

Mr. and Mrs. Gordon's wooden-framed home lay just beyond a thick copse of trees. Even on the darkest night, the woods prevented one house from seeing the other's lights.

"Hurry!"

"We will, Colleen."

Rebecca and her little sister ran as quietly and quickly as possible to the top of the staircase, ready to dash to the Gordon's home. At the last second, Rebecca glanced back, her heart heavy, knowing Colleen had the hardest task of all.

Chapter 10
Planning the Details

Rebecca held Hannah's hand tightly, both for reassurance that the child was still with her and to help calm her sister's fears. Rain hit their skin like pebbles. Thunder boomed over their heads, almost deafening them. Only the lightning flashes helped. They let off enough brilliant light that the girls had no trouble seeing where to go.

To Rebecca's surprise, lights still glowed in the kitchen of the Gordon home.

She pounded the door but barely had time for a second round when the door flew open, and there stood...garden boy!

"You! What are you doing here?" Rebecca knew she sounded churlish, but an image of Colleen sitting alone with their dead father not far away threw her into a near panic.

"I'm studying with Peter. What are you—two—doing here in the middle of the night?" He saw Hannah tucked in next to Rebecca and waved them in. A strong wind buffeted the panel, so he had to lean against it to close the door.

"Mr. Gordon." Hannah literally threw herself into the older man's arms.

Mr. Gordon handed Hannah off to his wife, then turned a worried face to Rebecca. "What's going on, Miss Rebecca? Midnight in a storm... This child's tears... What's wrong?" he asked, knowing only a crisis would send them out in such a storm. "Miss, are you wearing your dressing gown?" He looked behind Rebecca. "Where's Miss Colleen? Has something happened to her?"

"It's...it's..." Rebecca threw repeated glances at the young man next to her. How could she explain what was needed if he—a stranger—still stood here?

"It's too late to worry about Thomas. He's here, and he can help if needs be. Tell me what's happened."

"How can I trust him? I don't know him," Rebecca whispered, her glances bouncing back and forth between younger and older man.

"Miss Rebecca, get hold of yourself," the man almost bellowed. "There's a crying child in my wife's arms and you both soaked from head to boot. Clearly, something is wrong. Now get on to it."

Shocked out of her panic, Rebecca blurted, "Papa came home early. I spoke to him in the kitchen. Hannah had a tummy ache, and I was taking things back there. He seemed fine. No...no. He was distracted. Worried. Seemed to have something heavy on his mind. I heard a thump not long after that. I was in bed, but got up, thinking someone might be in the house. I got Colleen, and we looked around but found nothing. Thinking maybe Mama or Hannah fell out of bed, we checked on them. They were sleeping. So we checked on Papa. We hadn't bothered him because...well, I suppose...I thought he needed rest, and it *was* just one thump I heard.

But then..." She ran out of words. How to tell what they found?

"Papa died. Right there in his bedroom. Fell on the floor." Hannah finished the tale while still sitting on Mrs. Gordon's lap.

"What!" their audience gasped simultaneously.

"And now we need to call the doctor, bury Papa, and keep it a secret until Rebecca's birthday, so Uncle Eugene and Cousin Ross won't move in." Hannah had to take a huge breath after that long sentence said all at once.

"What!" the other three repeated.

Dropped jaws, wide eyes, and shaking heads were all Rebecca could see.

"Oh, my lord." Mrs. Gordon gathered Hannah again. While the child allowed the hug, she was without tears now.

"This isn't some tale Miss Colleen's invented, is it? You know she's come up with some good ones in the past." Mr. Gordon squinted one eye and looked down his nose at Rebecca.

"Swear to God, Mr. Gordon. I'm not...we're not lying. Papa's dead, and Uncle Eugene will talk Mama into letting him and his son move in. You know he will."

"True," the man admitted reluctantly, rubbing his jaw. "That's a crafty snake if ever I saw one. I always wondered how him and Mrs. Felicity came from the same mother and father."

"Please, Mr. Gordon, we need help, and we need it fast. We need Doctor Vincent to sign one of those papers that says when Papa died. We need Mrs. Gordon to sit in the hall in case Mama wakes up before...before we move Papa's body. And we need to bury him in this storm while it's night and no one's around." She turned and gave Thomas a hard glare.

"And we all need to keep this a secret, even from Mama, until my birthday."

"Which is—" started Thomas.

"Never mind when it is—it's not long off. But we have to delay until then, so I won't be forced to marry Cousin Ross, and Uncle won't frighten Mama into an early death."

"But Miss Rebecca, burying a man without a word to anyone. Isn't that illegal?"

"Is it? We are burying Papa on our property after the doctor writes his paper. I can run the business, and we can fend off my uncle and cousin as long as we have to. As long as no one wants to see Papa in person."

"We can do this, Mr. Gordon." Hannah got off Mrs. Gordon's lap and took the gardener's hand. "But we must hurry, or I'll be sent to boarding school, and Colleen will be sent far away."

"What?"

Rebecca took his other hand, pleading with him. "You know that's what will happen."

"Well, I suppose it can, yes." The old man gave his wife a helpless look.

"We have to keep the girls and Mrs. Felicity safe, husband."

"All right then. We need a plan. Give me a minute to think."

Silence fell inside as the storm raged outside.

"Right," Mr. Gordon finally said. "Thomas, grab your gear and high boots. Get the shovel and one of those weather lanterns. Remember the pile of wood we cut into cords last week?"

"Yes, sir."

"Do what you have to do in this storm to dig a deep grave

just near that stack. We'll lay the cordwood across the grave so it's not visible if anyone...or anything—comes looking. I'll take the mare and fetch Doctor Vincent. God knows how I'll explain this, but we need to keep the family safe from those two vultures. I hope he comes. Charlotte, gear up, and go up to the house. Take the girls with you. When me and the doctor are finished with what he needs to do, Thomas and I will move Mr. Robert's body. Thomas, you hustle that digging, and meet me on the back porch. We'll have to go sock footed through the house. Mrs. Felicity would notice muddy boot prints for sure and ask a dozen questions." He turned to each as he spoke. "Miss Rebecca, you take Miss Hannah, and go with Mrs. Gordon to the house. Be quiet as mice. When we leave for the woods, you three girls will go, too. Stand as witnesses along with Thomas, my wife and myself. This storm will help cover what we do, but it won't last forever."

Saying that, he hustled everyone out the door. Thomas headed around the house to the shed. Peter Gordon headed to the barn, running with his coat hugged close and one hand holding his hat tight to his head. Mrs. Gordon took the girls by the hands, and the three ran back to the house. The problem seemed to have a solution—however odd or legal— but the night was moving on, and so much remained to be done.

Chapter 11
Working the Plan

Colleen practically fell into Rebecca's arms when the girls returned to the house. She broke into ragged sobs but quickly swallowed them and used the sleeve of her dressing gown to wipe tears off her cheeks and snot from her nose.

"I thought you would never return." Never one to demonstrate emotion so much and fewer times to touch others, Colleen hugged Mrs. Gordon so hard the woman grunted.

"Off with you now." She patted Colleen and motioned her to stand with her sisters. "The bunch of you misses stay put. I am getting a chair and put by Mrs. Felicity's door. God forbid that woman wake up now, but she usually sleeps well into the morning." Mrs. Gordon sniffed and wiped her own nose. "She's not as spry as once she was." On that comment, she hustled into Hannah's room—it being the closest—and returned carrying a small vanity chair.

"I'll just sit here and pray, if you ladies don't mind."

"Prayers might be in order tonight. What with Papa..."

Hannah stopped but finished her thought. "What with Papa going to Heaven and all."

Rebecca figured that probably wasn't what she intended to say, but the thought was a nice one. She took each girl by the hand and offered a prayer. "Father, forgive us for what we are about to do. We may get in trouble, but we think it is for the best. Watch over those who are helping us. We pray Mama sleeps through all this. The worry about Papa and the future might prove too much otherwise. I never thought I would ask this, but Lord, could you let this storm rage on for a bit longer? We really need to hide what we're doing. Oh, not that we are doing anything wrong, but it's just that...well, other folks if they saw might not understand." She squeezed the two hands, and they intoned *amen* together.

With nothing to do but wait for Mr. Gordon and the doctor, the three slid down the wall and sat huddled. Hannah's nightgown hem dripped. She'd not held it up as they went to and from the Gordon's house.

"Sweetheart, go into your room and change. We have to go out again, but the rain is chilling. Do you have a pair of those dungarees that Hattie brought you?"

Hannah nodded and stood. "That will be more comfortable than a soggy nightgown." She opened the door to her room but stopped. "May I leave the door open so I can see you?"

"Certainly, you may."

While Hannah changed, Rebecca urged Colleen to do the same. "The weather is wild outside. Normally we would all be in bed and pay little attention, but just for tonight, we need this kind of storm. However, you will do better in that shorter skirt and boots than in your nightgown. But hurry, please. I would like to change as well before the men get here."

Colleen must have moved like a dervish through dressing. She and Hannah returned to the hall at the same time.

"Right. I'll dash to my room and change. Stay here, and hang on to each other," she said for Hannah's sake, as Colleen normally did not reach out to others like Rebecca did.

She did not think herself slow in dressing, but Mr. Gordon must have flown to the doctor's house and back, because he and Doctor Vincent were coming up the staircase as Rebecca returned to the hallway.

"Oh, thank you, Doctor!" Rebecca grabbed the elder man's hand in both of hers. "I don't know what Mr. Gordon told you, but we're in a bad way here."

"Gordon explained everything. I cannot say I agree with the plan, but I also don't care for Eugene Callaway. I brought all three of you young ladies into this world. I am not inclined to see you being mishandled by a man such as your uncle."

When it looked like all three girls would swarm him with gratitude, he huffed and puffed, raising a hand to ward them off. "I understand time is of the essence. Let's get on with this. Gordon, with me."

Doctor Vincent and Mr. Gordon disappeared into Robert Gilpin's bedroom, while the girls and Mrs. Gordon remained in the hall. A good ten minutes passed before the men returned. The doctor waved a paper at Rebecca. "I advise you to put this some place safe, young lady. There will be questions later when this all comes to light. And," he paused to glance back to the closed door, "I am staying. Going with you lot to the grave. Be a witness to this man's death and burial."

"Will you speak something over Papa's grave, sir?" Hannah stepped forward, once more demonstrating an innate ability to see a situation clearly.

Doctor Vincent laid a hand on her shoulder. "Would you like that, Miss Hannah?"

"Yes, please."

"Then I shall, just for you." He touched her cheek and raised sad eyes to the others. "When will we—"

"As soon as Thomas gets here, Doctor." Mr. Gordon inclined his head at a sound below stairs. "I think the youngun' is coming now."

Thomas took the staircase two steps at a time—in sock feet as Mr. Gordon said—and stopped next to the older man.

"Doctor Vincent, this is Thomas Willey. He's visiting with Mrs. Gordon and me, learning about plants and such. Thomas, this is the village doctor." The two men shook hands, and for a second or two, all stood around without moving.

"Best get on to it, Mr. Gordon," said Mrs. Gordon from her post. "This storm won't last forever, and the doctor needs to return home as soon as possible before someone else comes looking for him. And these young ladies need to get some rest. This ain't been the best of nights." She used a hand to shoo the men to work.

"Right. Uh, Thomas, I need your help."

Poor Thomas stood with wide eyes and stiff limbs.

"You never seen a dead person, have you, son?" Mr. Gordon asked kindly. "This might be the first, but I would bet it won't be the last." He laid a hand on the tall young man's shoulder. "But I hope it is."

"I'll go with you, just to make sure all is in order," the doctor said.

Thomas might have gulped loudly, but no one heard because of the noisy storm outside. Rebecca could see he really did not want to enter that room. However, the two older men would have trouble doing what needed to be done —moving Papa's body out of the house, through a raging storm to a grave somewhere in the acres behind the house.

Mr. Gordon took the young man's arm, and together the three entered the room, closing the door quietly behind them. Once more, the girls waited.

"I think we need to go downstairs and put on our gear and boots." Rebecca did not want to be in the hall when they returned with the body. That image was not something she wanted her sisters to remember.

"I'll stay." Hannah did not appear ready to abandon her father.

"Not me. I don't want to be around when they come out." Colleen almost ran to the staircase.

"Come, dear. We don't need to be here." Rebecca turned Hannah's shoulders and literally guided her down the hall. She almost had to drag Hannah down to the kitchen where Colleen already stood in cape, hat, and boots, rocking side to side, her anxiety plain to see.

"Hurry up, Hannah. We need to be ready when they come down."

No sooner did Colleen say that than Doctor Vincent came into view. "Ladies, please turn, and face the other way. Hold tight, and don't turn around until I tell you to."

At first, Rebecca thought him being bossy, but quickly it dawned on her that the old man did not want them to see Papa carried out.

She turned Hannah and pulled the little girl's back against her front. With one hand on Hannah, Rebecca reached out and pulled Colleen to her side, anchoring her so that her adventurous sister would not yield to temptation and see something she would never be able to un-see.

However much she protected the girls, hiding Colleen's face against her shoulder and covering Hannah's eyes, Rebecca saw reflected in the cabinet glass a man, carrying a bundle over his shoulder. The weight—a rug, probably with the body inside—must have been great or awkward because the other two men held Thomas' arms as he came slowly down the back staircase. The trio made slow progress across the kitchen and onto the porch.

"Miss Rebecca, please do not turn around. Can you wait here until Thomas comes for you all? You do not know where we are going—I don't even know. But we shan't be long. Then we can say farewell to your father. Will you wait?" Dr. Vincent touched her arm as he asked them to wait.

"Yes, sir. We'll wait." Rebecca pushed Colleen's head back onto her shoulder and squeezed Hannah's shoulder as a shiver ran through the small body.

"Count to one hundred, Miss, then you can all sit until Thomas returns."

The three counted aloud together, Rebecca keeping the count steady and accurate.

Eventually, they came to one hundred and turned around. Nothing in the room seemed different. Thunder still boomed, as threatening as ever. Lightning still flashed like fireworks going off. Beyond those flashes, the darkness remained, as black and sinister as ever.

Chapter 12
Carrying Out the Plan

"Misses, follow me, please." Thomas still wore his long, wet coat, his cap dripping on to the tiles of the back porch. He stood at the French doors, holding one open, waving them to come. "The doctor and Mr. Gordon don't need to be out in this weather any longer than necessary. But they won't start the service until you arrive."

He said *service* as if this were a normal funeral, done in daylight with loved ones ringing the grave. This was anything but normal. Rebecca came out of her stupor and hustled her sisters out of the door. Thomas stayed ahead of them but went slowly enough into the underbrush, so they never lost sight of him.

He led them much further back into their property than Rebecca thought he would.

Of course, she thought. *They must be careful where they lay Papa. No one must stumble onto the grave and question what or who.* She held Hannah's hand and sometimes pulled just to make the girl hurry.

"Over here, miss." Thomas waved them to a thick cope of trees, a single lantern throwing abysmal light in a tiny circle. If Rebecca hadn't known they were going to stop at a gravesite, she would have wondered why they stopped here.

"Your father is here, Miss Rebecca." She didn't see anything indicating a recent grave until she noticed leaves scattered in a tight area around where she stood. Unable to speak, she simply nodded and pulled her sisters to her side.

Rain pounded harder, determined, it seemed, to drown out the doctor's words. She would never remember them, half-heard words of comfort that defied reality.

"Miss Rebecca." Mr. Gordon had to lean close to her in order for her to hear. Thunder bounced off the very trees. Lightning illuminated the woods, the trees with their fresh summer dressing ominous in the flashing glow. "Do you want to say something?"

What? Say something? The reality seemed so dreamlike. She could barely wrap her head around the fact that they stood in pouring rain with dangerous lightning popping around them as thunder deafened them. What was she supposed to say? *Why did you die? What am I supposed to do now? Mama can't handle this. She will crumble. Everything falls on me to handle. What do I do now?*

"Where... Where does he lie?" she finally came out of the mental fog enough to ask.

"Here, miss. Just here." Mr. Gordon pointed at a particularly small pile of leaves, so innocuous in appearance.

Rebecca leaned over, picked up some loose soil, held it up at arm's level then let it trickle out of her hand onto her father's grave. "Bye, Papa. I love you."

Colleen imitated her, though Rebecca could not tell if she said anything.

Hannah slipped her hand into Rebecca's. "Do I have to?"

"No, Hannah. You don't. Papa will understand."

Hannah dropped her eyes but nodded. "Can we go home now?" The lightning moved aside for the child's heart-breaking question.

"I think it best. Doctor, Mr. Gordon, you are finished here?" Rebecca asked.

"The doctor will return with you and Thomas," Mr. Gordon said. "But the lad must come back. We still have something to do here."

Stack the cords of wood over Papa's grave so no person—or animal—can find it. She knew enough about death to know that final state drew animals.

"Very well. Let's go home." She took the girls' hands, and Thomas led them and Doctor Vincent back to the house.

"Thank you, sir, for coming out on such a sad occasion," Rebecca said as she shook his hand. "If we owe you—"

"No, no, Miss Rebecca. There is no charge. It appears your father died of a heart attack, possibly caused by the stress of traveling so much." The doctor touched the bill of his hat, the edges running with rainwater, and climbed into his buggy.

She turned to Thomas. She included him now in those who had a vital secret to keep. She held out her hand to him. "Garden boy—Thomas—I trust you to keep your word about this. I can't imagine what life will be like if our relatives find out about Papa. Thank you for your help. That had to be most difficult."

"I'm glad I was there to help. If you need me, simply look for me in the gardens." With that, Thomas, too, tugged his cap in salute and disappeared into the night.

"Come, girls. We need to prepare for morning." Rebecca

led the way into the kitchen, leaving their boots on the back porch. They had shaken out their capes and left them in the washroom for Hattie to clean.

"Prepare? How do you mean?" Colleen led the way up the stairs but stopped on the landing to find out what her sister had in mind.

"First, we relieve Mrs. Gordon. That's part of the plan for keeping our secret." Rebecca led the way up. The woman dozed. "Mrs. Gordon?"

"Huh? Oh, Miss Rebecca. Is it done?"

"Yes, your husband, the doctor, and...Thomas handled it so well, we merely showed up to say our farewells to Papa. But we must get you back home before Mr. Gordon begins to worry." Rebecca held out a hand and helped the woman ease up out of the chair where she had sat for hours, while Hannah and Colleen moved down the hall to their bedrooms. As soon as Mrs. Gordon was stable on her feet, Rebecca turned to her own room.

"Miss?"

"Yes?"

"Tomorrow..."

All three girls stopped, but Rebecca answered. "Yes? What about tomorrow?"

"We should...you know...tidy up your father's room and put away his suitcase. His bed will need a new cover. Things like that. Hattie won't touch the room unless one of us asks. So we'll be all right there."

"You're right. There are things in Papa's room that need straightening. I can do that."

"No, miss. Pardon, but you shouldn't be doing that kind of thing. I've dealt with the days after death and know what to look for and how to handle it."

The girls had no idea to what she referred, but Rebecca nodded. "Whatever you think is best. Thank you."

"I'm sorry your father died, misses. He was a good man. And for what it's worth, I think he would have approved of your plan."

Unable to speak, Rebecca nodded again and followed Hannah into her room. "Shall I sit with you, sister, until you fall asleep?"

"Yes, please."

Time passed quickly, and Hannah fell asleep in less than five minutes. Rebecca eased out of the child's room and stepped over to Colleen's room. With a knock, she pushed the door open a little and called out in a soft voice, "May I come in?"

"Yes. Sleep eludes me anyway, just when I want it badly." Colleen sat propped up in bed, her face wan in the soft light of a candle on the commode beside her.

"Are you feeling all right, Colleen?"

"You ask that after what we have been through? I cannot imagine how anyone would say *yes, fine* after seeing your father dead on the floor and attending a crude burial somewhere deep in a forest in the middle of the night in the middle of a storm."

"When you put it that way, you are absolutely correct. None of us is fine. You look so pale, though. Are you feeling poorly like Hannah did earlier? Before—"

"No." Colleen ran a hand over her face, perhaps to wipe off sweat. One arm lay over her stomach as if she did indeed suffer some sort of ache. "I am tired and sick at heart. Our future depends on a secret that too many share. Including a boy we know nothing about."

"Mr. Gordon vouches for him."

"True, and that is the only reason I am not running away from home before Uncle can send me somewhere." Colleen glanced up at Rebecca and read her thoughts. "You are right, you know. Uncle doesn't care for my *bold attitude*. He has said as much before. Quietly, on the sly, to me. And he's not fond of children either. Hannah and I will be out the door if he comes to stay. Mama, bless her heart, is a weak woman." Colleen smirked.

Rebecca opened her mouth to protest, but Colleen cut her off. "I love her dearly, but she is, and we both know it. And when it comes to Uncle Eugene, she grew up adoring him as her older brother and probably still thinks like that to some extent. No matter. Uncle is a con man who wraps others around his finger and makes them think *they* have done *him* a favor."

"You're being a bit cynical tonight, but I suppose it is warranted."

"Warranted or not, we must play this game we have started and hope nothing happens to expose us. Though..." Colleen fell silent, her arm still wrapped around her middle.

Her silence waved a red flag like a bullfighter. Colleen seldom left anything unsaid and the gloomier, the more often she carried on too much.

"Sister, you have a problem." Rebecca's words came out as a statement, not a question.

Colleen sat snuggled in bed, focused on something other than this particular night, Rebecca guessed.

"Yes." Colleen dragged out the word but did not look at her sister.

"There is a solution?"

More seconds passed. "Yes, but time must pass first."

"Is that meant to be perplexing, or are you being obtuse?"

"Neither. I speak the plain truth."

"And you will not share this problem?"

"Forgive me, I am rather tired now." Colleen scooted down in her bed, turned on her side away from her sister, leaned over, and blew out the candle.

Rebecca stood in the dark, the storm's noise and fury fading but not entirely gone. Perhaps it was the pounding rain that made her sister's action ominous. Shivers ran down her back, but she could not say why as she stepped back to the door.

"Goodnight, sister."

Out of the dark came a strong but quiet voice. "I will tell you, Rebecca. But in my own time. It's not an easy problem to share. Know that I love you, though. And I trust you. Goodnight."

What is there to say to that? Something is wrong, or she would have asked for my help immediately. Still, she says she'll tell me. For tonight perhaps, that is as good as I can expect.

The door closed quietly, only the snick of the lock sounding in the hall.

———

Mama came downstairs well after the girls had their breakfast the next morning. Even they slept late, but Mrs. Gordon had the meal ready and strong coffee for Rebecca.

Before leaving the dining room after breakfast, Hannah approached Rebecca. "I'm scared, Rebecca." She rarely admitted being scared. The courage and clean-sightedness of the previous night must have faded with daylight and a realization of what had happened in the dark.

Rebecca wrapped an arm around Hannah and hugged

her. "We're all scared, sweetheart. What if we say something and Mama—or even Hattie—begins to wonder about Papa? Being as the weather is lovely perhaps for as long as you can, you might enjoy being outside. Yes..." She held up a hand, anticipating her little sister's worry. "You have to read to Mama, but later. You know she often falls asleep soon after you begin. The sound of your voice is very soothing." The compliment brought a smile to Hannah's face. "If Mama wants to talk, answer her, but simply do not volunteer anything other than what she mentions. Don't look so sad. She *will* ask you what is troubling you if she sees such a gloomy face." She leaned down and caught Hannah's down-cast gaze. "You can do this, Hannah."

Hannah nodded but kept her head down. "May I be excused?"

"Yes, you may."

"Well, that takes care of her, but what about me?" Colleen sat at the table, her hands folded in front of her. Hattie had cleared the table while the girls sat finishing their drinks.

"Mama seldom moves from the parlor. She joins us for lunch and sometimes dinner, but you know that she only comes down that late if Papa is home. She still thinks he's traveling." She shifted sideways in her chair to face Colleen more squarely.

"I've been thinking. It's true that he's been gone longer than usual. Mama, bless her heart, seldom pays attention to calendars. I may contrive to send Papa to California in search for some Oriental jewels that have come to his attention. That should buy us another three weeks."

"She will expect a letter, you know," Colleen reminded her.

"Humm, yes. I'll think of something."

"That takes care of Papa, but what about me?" Colleen repeated, as if her sister might have forgotten how important each person's role was in the coming days.

"Let me think. You can't spend all day outdoors like Hannah. Perhaps you have friends you can visit? Or go to the lending library in the village? Or run errands for Mrs. Gordon?"

"All well and good, but that won't keep me busy for weeks, and you well know that." Colleen sat with that far-off expression on her face that Rebecca saw often lately.

"You're up to something, Colleen. I can tell."

"What?" Colleen turned innocent eyes on her sister.

"When you get that look, you're up to no good."

"I had a marvelous idea for keeping me away from Mama. And it might be kind of fun at that."

"And what might that be, if I may be so bold as to ask?"

"I'll tell you when I've worked it all out." Colleen pushed her chair back and stood, brushing a few wrinkles out of her skirt.

"Don't give me that innocent look. You do that when you're at your worst. That's two things now that you're going to tell me about, sister." Rebecca cocked an eyebrow and gave her sister a warning glare.

"Oh, is it?" Colleen walked quickly out of the dining room before Rebecca could try prying more information out of her.

"Innocent miss, my foot." Rebecca watched Colleen sashay out the door, then forgot her worries about her middle sister and turned to her own.

Chapter 13
Mama Rises to the Occasion

"Well, damn!" Colleen shouted.

All three girls happened to meet in the front foyer an hour later, just in time to see a buggy coming toward the house, winding among the oaks that lined the wide drive.

Rebecca threw her hands over Hannah's ears. "Colleen Amanda Gilpin! Wherever did you learn that word?"

Hannah pushed off Rebecca's hands and leaned forward in order to see better. "Golly! It's Uncle Eugene and—oh dear—Cousin Ross." Hannah turned fearful eyes up to Colleen and Rebecca. "Does he know?"

"You mean about Papa?" Rebecca whispered after checking to see if Mama or Hattie were around. "No one's said anything. I think they're here to make trouble as usual."

"I wish just once Cousin Ross would say something indelicate to me so I could punch him in the nose," Colleen said, stepping back from the window as the buggy pulled up in front of the porch.

"That's bloodthirsty, sister. And swearing too. Papa

would swat your backside, and Mama would faint." Rebecca smoothed her hair, a nervous habit rather than primping for a prospective beau.

"Who the hell do you think taught me that word?" Colleen turned a nasty smirk on Rebecca. "Papa said it all the time. No one swatted him, and I never saw Mama faint when he used it."

Their words might have turned into an argument on etiquette or Papa's and Mama's behavior, but the sound of heavy boots approaching the door stopped them.

A knock sounded, and Hattie came flying around the corner from the parlor.

"Oh good." Rebecca sighed. "Hattie, count to twenty, then admit the men to the parlor. Mama will see them there."

The maid nodded, and Rebecca shooed the other two ahead of her. "We won't leave Mama's side unless she sends us out. Pray she is strong today." Rebecca shot a meaningful glance at Colleen who nodded in understanding.

———

"Brother, you simply don't understand," Mama said, sipping her weak tea. "Robert deals in matters that take him far and wide." She'd told Rebecca years before that she had never explained to her brother what her husband's job involved, more to protect him and the valuables he traded in rather than keep secrets.

"But, Sister, you are alone here." Eugene sat forward in his chair, his hand out, an anxious expression on his face.

As if he cares. Rebecca kept a straight face, happy to see Colleen did as well. Mama had sent Hannah out of the room as soon as they had all shared greetings. Uncle's blatant manipulations had begun the minute he entered the room, but today Cousin Ross remained quiet, his attention on Mama. His stare skewered her like a butterfly to a board. Alive and still flapping.

Mama repeated what she said when Eugene first brought up her husband's absence. "Robert travels a great deal. He writes often. I am never alone. My daughters are here, as well as my gardener, his helper, our maid, and the cook." She blithely replaced her cup, folded her hands in her lap, and gazed at her brother as if that explanation closed the topic.

Eugene sat forward, gathered her hands in his, and lowered his voice to a sickeningly sweet tone. "That is indeed true, my sweet. But you are not safe, even surrounded as you are by other females and elderly men." He eased forward even further, caught her gaze, and held it like a snake charmer, using his smooth voice and lower tones to hypnotize his sister. "Ross and I can stay with you while Robert travels. We can leave when he returns home. I—we—are only thinking of the family's safety and well-being."

"Papa should be here any day now," Rebecca said. "I doubt he will be happy to see relatives have made themselves at home in his absence." She spoke without one ounce of maidenly blush or female softness. She meant to stop this invasion, if possible.

"That's true, Eugene." Mama pulled her hands out of her brother's grasp and gave Rebecca a smile that she normally reserved only for her husband. "We really don't need your assistance." Seeing a frown gather between her brother's brows, she quickly added, "But we are much obliged for you thinking of us. We shall call on your kind offer if ever we are in need."

Colleen winked at Rebecca, though careful not to let the

others see.

We avoided their attempt to conquer this time, Rebecca thought, relieved. *However, Mama seems determined to keep peace with her brother.*

"Why don't you and Ross stay for lunch?" Mama offered. "We shall dine under the trees. It's too lovely a day to stay inside. That way we can walk around the house, and you can see our gardens as you prepare to leave."

Startled by the directions of her mother's comments, Rebecca wasn't sure if her mother won the battle or not. Did Mama's inviting the despicable pair to stay for lunch wipe out any advantage she gained by refusing Eugene's offer of help? However, Rebecca mused, Mama did inform the pair that they would be leaving afterwards...by viewing the gardens on the way to their buggy.

We will breathe easier when Uncle and Cousin Ross actually leave. The day those two arrive with suitcases in hand is the day trouble walks in the door, and we're doomed.

Rebecca and Colleen stood when their mother did. Uncle Eugene moved to Mama's side as if to escort her to the dining room. However, Mama sidetracked him.

"Rebecca, dear, may I speak to you privately for a moment? Colleen, would you escort our guests outside, please?"

"Yes, Mama." Rebecca moved to Mama's other side and held out her arm.

"Yes, Mama." Colleen moved to the double doors, opened them, and waited with an exaggeratedly innocent expression on her face.

Sister might hate leading those two out of here, but she's smart enough to know Mama managed to avoid contact with Uncle, Rebecca thought.

Uncle Eugene looked like a thundercloud for about ten seconds, while Ross smirked. But both turned on their heels and passed Colleen, who winked at Rebecca and her mother.

When the two were alone, Mama squeezed Rebecca's arm. "You don't care for my brother very much. And that's all right. But Cousin Ross is a fine-looking man with his own fortune to bring to a marriage, dear."

With a small groan, Rebecca realized Mama may have put off Uncle Eugene, but she played matchmaker, turning her attention to her eldest daughter.

"I'm not ready to marry, Mama. I am Papa's bookkeeper and needed here while he travels. You said he travels so much. Ross won't wait forever to marry, and I'm not really interested in marrying a cousin."

Mama patted her daughter's hand and moved her toward the door. "Perhaps you will change your mind. After all, you are almost *on the shelf,* as Eugene said not long ago."

"Shelf or not, Mama, I do not want to marry Ross." Why couldn't Mama understand that Ross was not desirable, regardless of appearance or wealth? Additionally, Papa had once put forth the idea that Uncle Eugene and Ross might not be as wealthy as they made out to be.

Lunch came and went with idle conversation, mainly between the brother and sister. Mama managed to avoid mention of marriage or her daughters other than to praise how beautiful and sweet they were. The girls—Hannah included—sat silent, answering only when addressed directly and only in short manner.

Poor Colleen and Hannah might as well be invisible. Uncle and Cousin Ross pay no attention to them at all. Thankfully, neither uncle nor cousin pay much attention to me either, Rebecca mused as courses came and went.

The pair focused on complimenting Mama in one breath and worrying about the family's safety in another, all in condescending terms. They implied no one on the property had the ability to take care of themselves, much less each other. Rebecca had to pinch Colleen under the tablecloth in order to keep her quiet. Even Rebecca grew angry at their insinuations.

Only Mama standing, signaling the end of the meal, relieved Rebecca's nerves. Like a queen, her mother offered her arm to her brother. Ross offered his to Rebecca who, forced by good manners, took it. However, she refused to either look directly at him or speak to him. Mama gushed over her flowers, rarely giving Uncle Eugene time to speak. Not soon enough as far as Rebecca was concerned, the group arrived at the front drive where Mr. Gordon held the reins of their horse.

One last time, Uncle Eugene attempted to manipulate his sister into letting him and his son move in.

"I'm sorry, Eugene. Robert will be upset finding others in his home. We shall visit again, I know. Pleasant trip to you and Ross."

Seeing they could not bully their way into the household, both placed a dutiful kiss on Mama's cheek and tipped their hats to the girls. Ross moved to kiss Rebecca's cheek, but she took a large step back, giving him a frown to reinforce her lack of enthusiasm for the maneuver.

With nothing else to hold the two there, the men drove off. Mama turned to her daughters, wobbling a bit. Rebecca rushed to one side and Colleen to the other.

"Mama? Are you all right?" Hannah turned a fearful face up to her mother.

"Yes, dear. I'm so very tired though. Eugene's visits do

wear me out so. Perhaps I'll just rest now, if you three will excuse me. I'll take a tray in my room for dinner."

"You're really all right, Mama?" Perhaps Hannah feared her mother's demise, the image of a stormy funeral all too fresh in her mind's eye.

"Yes, my darling." Mama reached out and brushed a hand down her little girl's face. "I just need a nap. Girls, would you assist me? Perhaps you all might sit with me until I fall asleep?"

"Yes, Mama."

———

"What did Mama want with you after we left?" Colleen waited until the three left the room, and Hannah slipped into her room for a doll.

"She played matchmaker for Cousin Ross and myself, insinuating that he is handsome and wealthy and would make a fine match."

"Oh yes, I forgot the comment Uncle made about you being on the shelf."

"I had too, but Mama apparently had not."

"What did she whisper to you just now before we left her room?"

At this, Rebecca sighed and stopped at the balcony over-looking the front foyer. "She wanted to know when Papa would return. She said he hasn't written in ever so long."

"Oh dear. Count on Mama to be aware of his letters, but not the exact passage of time."

"True."

"So what are you going to do about a letter?"

"I know what *you* would do."

Colleen had the grace to lift a brow, though not apologize. "I'd grab paper and pen and get on with it."

With one hand stuffed into her skirt pocket and the other knuckled under her chin, Rebecca gave in and agreed. "Mama expects a letter. Thankfully, I write so very much like Papa, and I always get the mail. She only gets Papa's letters, so she'll never know there was no post mark on the envelope."

"I think it best if Mama gets a *letter* from *Papa*. She'll forget about his absence in the excitement of hearing from him."

Both stood silent, waiting for Hannah to appear.

"What a pack of lies we're mounting up," Colleen added as she rubbed her stomach. "I wish it were otherwise, but I do not relish traveling from here to who-knows-where at Uncle's bidding."

"Ready to go outside?" Hannah walked down the hall toward them, her favorite doll in hand.

"Are you taking Molly Sue for a breath of fresh air, sweetheart?" Rebecca stepped onto the staircase on one side of Hannah and Colleen took up the other side.

"I think she's been cooped up too long. I enjoyed being outside at lunch, though I didn't enjoy lunch." The child paused and sent her sisters a grin. "That sounded odd, but you know what I mean."

Both older girls laughed. "Indeed, we do, Hannah. You take your dolly outside, and enjoy it this time. And do be careful that Rags doesn't run away with Molly Sue." Colleen tweaked a loose hair next to Hannah's cheek. "The sun and garden will do you good."

"Indeed," said Hannah, sounding so much like Colleen that the middle daughter broke into laughter.

Chapter 14
A Gentle, Necessary Lie

A sunny, warm day deserved attention. Other than a walk that morning and a visit with Mr. Gordon as well as Thomas, Rebecca sat in her usual place in Papa's office, staring at letters, bills, requests, and the open account book.

I enjoyed visiting with Thomas this morning, Rebecca mused. *He's not much older than I and plans to attend college. I wish I were that bold. But I think life has other plans for me... at least until such time as Colleen and Hannah marry. At least Colleen. Hannah, Mama, and I can manage with the help of the Gordons and Hattie. Colleen worries me lately, though. Something's not right. Her problem, as she said. I wish she'd share. Perhaps she can't come up with a solution. But between us, we should be able to.*

She wasn't trying to put off taking care of the morning business. She wanted time to enjoy peace and quiet for a change. The younger girls had ventured into the village, to the lending library and to pick up several things for Mrs.

Gordon from the green grocer. Before returning home, they would stop by the postal office for the daily mail.

Mama sat in the parlor, reading, something she did less these days. More and more she remained in bed, upright with a tray over her lap, eating there, reading, listening to Hannah read, writing to Papa, or napping. Her letters to Robert Gilpin remained in the bottom drawer of Rebecca's desk, in the only drawer that locked. Not that her mother would deign to snoop, but one never knew what a person might do if desperate.

Mama acted desperate now and then. She wanted her husband to return. A letter would satisfy her, but not forever. A letter...

Rebecca pulled a letter from under her ink blotter. Casting a glance at the door, she folded it, then wrote Mama's name and the home address. So similar was her writing to Papa's that no one—business or personal—knew the difference. Papa had often bragged that he could send her on one of his trips, to conduct a transaction of jewel exchange, and no one would question her signature or knowledge.

Reluctantly, Rebecca laid the letter on the corner of her desk. Though the village enjoyed getting mail in a box outside their home, that sort of delivery had not come to those outside the village boundaries yet. Colleen would pick up the Gilpin mail at the postal office. When the girls brought the daily mail back home, Rebecca would take "Papa's" letter to Mama.

These secrets—Papa's death, the number of those who knew of it, the girls' worries about both uncle and cousin— wore on her heart, her soul, and her conscience. Rebecca sometimes feared going to church on Sundays, worried that

God might smite her down for lying so much in such a short time.

Oddly enough, Mrs. Gordon's words about Papa approving of the girls' plans comforted Rebecca more than she thought it should.

While waiting to add more to her collection of soul-wrenching lies with Mama and the fake letter, Rebecca turned to the account book that showed wealth and a secure future. Papa's built-in safe contained several collections of rare jewels. Several letters in front of her confirmed interest in buying them for a hefty profit.

Papa always had a way of buying jewels at a cost far less than what he got for them at sale. He frequented places in port cities where immigrants came in to sell family jewelry that came over with them from the old country. He also checked estate sales in homes of the wealthy where no relative survived or the family became impoverished, which happened more often than imagined. Sons or husbands overspent on extravagant fun, then killed themselves in shame, leaving a grieving woman to find out the wealth was gone.

At one time, Rebecca thought her father's way of procuring some of his jewels rather cold-hearted, but soon understood that other jewel traders did the same thing. Papa did better than the majority of his competitors.

"I'm going upstairs, dear. I'll have my lunch there." Rebecca looked up to see Mama standing in the doorway, leaning on Hattie.

"May I do anything for you, Mama?"

"No, dear. Hattie can see me up and help me into bed. I'll dine off a tray, read a little, then nap. You can bring up the mail later. I'm sure your father's letter will be here any day, telling us where he is and what he's doing. You said he went to California?"

"I believe I did, yes."

"How exciting. But California is so far away."

"It is, Mama." Rebecca chose her words carefully, not willing to lead on her mother if she could help it. Not for the world would she tell Mama that Papa was coming home just to relieve her mother's anxiety. How long the girls could keep this up, she had no idea.

"Don't work too hard, dear," Mama said as she and Hattie turned away from the door.

"I'll see you later, Mama."

"Yes, dear," came faintly from the hallway beyond the office door.

———

"Is it terrible to lie? Lie to my mother?" Rebecca sat on a blanket near the peony bush, twisting grass into knots, while Thomas leaned on the rock wall nearby.

"Yes, it's terrible to lie." Thomas tossed a small pebble as he leaned against the rock wall, but he faced Rebecca's shocked expression bravely with an explanation. "A lie to ease a breaking heart is not truly a black lie. Is it better for your mother to go on living in ignorance of her husband's unexpected death or tell her when she already suffers ill health and could possibly suffer worse? I say lie gently, kindly." He gathered more pebbles, then turned back to her. "Your conscience must be suffering if you come to me to air your concerns. I'm a stranger here."

"Stranger to these parts perhaps—you have never said where you come from or where you plan to go to college.

You've never mentioned your family. But Thomas, anyone who buries my father in the middle of the night in the middle of a storm, as my sister Colleen pointed out, is no stranger to me. You perhaps more than anyone outside this family—and that includes the Gordons—are now part of us. And as we've visited over the past weeks, I find your views on subjects valuable."

Thomas blushed and tossed the handful of pebbles across the yard. "I like your sisters, you know. Hannah is a sweetheart. She'll bowl over some young man in a few years with her beauty, grace and charm. Colleen..." He let his words trail off, his gaze not meeting Rebecca's.

"You are at a loss for words when it comes to her. Most people are, you know." Rebecca laughed, tossing her handful of crushed leaves aside and leaning back on her hands. "Colleen is too smart by half, and she well knows it. She's capable of so many things yet has not found the one thing that awakens her passion. She's outspoken, outrageous, yet knows how to mind her manners and tongue when it suits her." Rebecca pulled her feet up and rested her arms across her covered knees. "At the moment, we all fear our uncle and cousin. We believe Uncle Eugene plans on moving in and taking care of Mama and me. He hasn't come right out and said so yet...but he will."

Thomas stood, his attitude showing how appalling the idea was. "What about your sisters?"

"Oh, Uncle has no use for either Colleen or Hannah. They will be shipped out so fast their bonnet strings will flap in the breeze." She turned her attention to the lake, so Thomas wouldn't see her tears.

"And you?" His voice came low, angry. As if he already knew her answer.

"What do you think?" She sat up, as angry as he appeared to be. "Cousin Ross will propose, pay two minutes of suit to my face but weeks of fawning in public then force me to marry him."

"He can't force you!"

"Oh, no? Threaten to send the girls away? Uncle will do that, not my cousin, so that would leave Ross' hands clean. Put Mama in a hospital for the weak or dying? Possibly. That would be something Eugene Callaway might do. Declare Mama incompetent to handle her own financial affairs and take over as her guardian with me married to Ross, with no say-so in the matter? Oh yes, Eugene and Ross Callaway are quite capable of doing just that."

Angry at the prospect, with no recourse for saving her family in sight but a birthday a month away, Rebecca stood, tossed the weeds off her skirt, and stomped. Not her typical behavior, but time held her hands tied. "If I can reach my birthday, then the bank and our lawyer have no recourse but to give me financial freedom. With that comes the right to choose my own husband—or not. I do not plan on spending my life tied to a man like Ross Callaway. Papa suspected Eugene and Ross of overstating their financial situation. Papa knew of several deals the two engaged in over the last few years that failed. So marrying me would give my uncle and cousin access and control of my monies. After all, a little woman isn't capable of taking care of herself, much less all that dirty old money." She patted her chest in mock drama as if she would faint and simpered when she spoke. Still angry, she spit as her papa had taught her to do when she was little —yet another secret from her mother.

Thomas looked challenged: laugh at Rebecca's unladylike behavior or stay angry on her behalf. Finally, he held up a hand as a sign for peace. "I ought to laugh at that, but I think I'll stay angry just a bit longer. I always want to think good of my fellow man, but the more I hear about those two, the less I like them. And the more concerned I am that they may try something dodgy between now and your birthday. When is it, so I can keep track of what's going on?"

She told him. They nodded to each other as though conspirators.

"Rebecca!" She turned toward the call.

"That's Hannah," Rebecca explained. "They've been out most of the day, visiting and running errands. They will have the mail as well. Mama is looking for a letter from Papa." Rebecca moved toward the house.

"But he's—"

"True, but Mama doesn't know that. And I can write like Papa, so..."

Thomas stuffed his hands in his pockets and joined her as she walked. "Lord, that must really be a trial for your heart."

"You have no idea." She stopped and turned to him. "I not only enjoy talking with you about life in general, but you help me see things straighter."

He seemed surprised by her statement, taking a step back as if he might be guilty of some crime. "Me? I don't do anything but listen."

"Listening is something Colleen does not do well. No one else is ready to stand by me and simply listen. I think..." She paused and gave him a long look that probably puzzled him. "By listening, you let me think aloud. That helps more than you know. Thank you."

She left him standing slack-jawed.

———

"Mama, I have a letter for you." She refrained from saying *from Papa* though she had to bite her tongue to stay quiet, as that was her usual way of bringing up the man's letters to his wife.

Mama clapped her hands, her face aglow, her eyes twinkling like a young girl receiving a letter from a beau. "I knew I'd get a letter today. How exciting!"

Rebecca handed over the one-page letter, each word tightly written in the way her father taught her. For a scant moment, she held her breath as her mother snatched the letter from her hand and began to read, her mouth saying each word without sound. So lost was the woman in reading that Rebecca slipped away, no longer able to bear Mama's happiness.

Later, Rebecca found herself confiding in her middle sister. "How can I tell her, Colleen? I'll break her heart."

The girls sat on the back porch, a soft breeze carrying tiny bugs that blinked off and on in the night's darkness.

"I don't envy you, sister. You are the one she will turn to eventually when there are no more excuses. He never stayed away so long, and she's aware of that on some level." Colleen held a tiny fan, its thin wooden ribs holding up paper limp with humidity. She slumped in a chair, waving the fan back and forth in an attempt to dry her perspiration.

"I'm aware of time passing, and with each day and no Papa arriving, her anxiety grows. I fear her mental health deteriorates as much as her physical. She has trouble walking these days."

"I noticed that," Colleen said quietly. "She rarely leaves her rooms anymore. And when she does, she must lean heavily on one of us or Hattie."

"What am I going to tell her if she asks why Papa hasn't come home yet?"

"Perhaps the truth will be easier than her thinking something has happened to him."

"Honestly? I can't imagine which would be worse—her knowing or her not knowing. Either way could kill her."

In typical Colleen fashion, she offered her final word on the topic: "I don't envy you, sister."

Chapter 15
Another Lie

The summer weather remained muggy after the Fourth of July. The family didn't go to the village but sat on the banks of the lake in order to see the annual fireworks. Mama, however, wasn't well enough to go downstairs, much less across the wide yard to the chairs set up for Hannah, Colleen, the Gordons, and Thomas. Hattie had thanked them earlier for asking her to join them, but she would celebrate with her family in the village.

Though her fiancé had died on July 4 the year before, Rebecca had always loved the day, with its stirring speeches, gatherings, friends, wonderful food and of course the fireworks. While the girls decided it best to stay close to home this year, she had looked forward to watching the bright colors rise, boom then float down to hiss in the lake's waters.

At the last minute, Mama asked Rebecca to sit with her on the balcony outside her room in the rear of the house. Reluctantly, she agreed. Together they could see the fireworks, but not the rise nor the fall. Just the top of each color.

Only the bright spots. On reflection, Rebecca mused that Mama was like that—only seeing the bright spots.

———

The summer continued on, edging closer to that fateful day when Rebecca could rightfully claim her inheritance and her freedom as well as her official place in the Gilpin business.

"Mama's not so well, is she?" Hannah turned a worried face to Rebecca one evening while they finished dinner. The little girl still read to her mother each afternoon. "She looks so pale and hardly speaks anymore."

"Mama worries. Sometimes she has reason, and sometimes I think she imagines things to worry about." Rebecca continued with her dessert, hoping the child would not ask for a more detailed explanation.

"She misses Papa and asks when he'll come home." After that, Hannah turned her focus onto her own dessert, her eyes down, her face drawn and pale.

Rebecca laid her spoon aside and put her hands in her lap. "Yes, dear, she does. What can I do to help her without telling her the truth? Will the truth help her get better?"

Hannah, the observant and wise, shook her head reluctantly, her gaze still on her dessert. "No."

"We are caught in a spider web of our own making—trying to keep Mama happy without admitting the truth which will hurt her."

"But it's hard lying to her, Rebecca," Hannah admitted.

"I know. I understand exactly how you feel. But I have no idea how to go forward if Mama gets worse."

With nothing else to say, they dropped the subject. But

Rebecca could tell the guilt of their secret ate on her sisters' hearts as much as it did on hers.

———

With three weeks to go before Rebecca's birthday, she wandered outside one sultry afternoon, looking for Colleen. The girl had avoided her for a week now, and she wanted to know why. Perhaps it was Colleen's secret problem?

"There you are." Rebecca found her sister sitting on a swing attached to a tall oak. They kept the swing in good condition because it faced the lake, and each enjoyed using it.

"Here I am." Colleen never took her view off the lake. Her voice sounded dreamy.

"Are you all right?"

"I suppose."

"What the devil does that mean?"

"Really, big sister. Such language."

"Don't give me that missy-type of innocence. You're avoiding me, and I want to know why." Rebecca came around to stand in front of Colleen where she sat, hands on the ropes, one foot pushing against the ground just enough to make the swing move back and forth.

"Innocence?" Colleen broke into laughter, loud, raucous, almost hysterical. "I would say *innocent* is the last thing you might think of me after..."

Her words ceased, and Rebecca craned her head forward as if urging Colleen to finish.

"After?"

"After I tell you a story. Remember that logical decision versus illogical one discussion we had in my room some months back?"

"I remember, but what does that have to do with why you're avoiding me?" Rebecca had just about enough of Colleen's meandering. She put a fist on each hip and demanded an explanation that made sense.

"Let me tell you a story."

"Oh, for goodness sake." Exasperated now, Rebecca threw up her hands and lifted her eyes as if seeking Divine strength to not throttling her sister on the spot. "Speak then. Tell me a story."

"Papa often said my sense of self-confidence is well-developed. Mama has praised me for my creativity, my resourcefulness. After Hannah cut her leg and I stayed with her, keeping her calm until help arrived, Papa complimented me, saying I was good under fire, like the old soldiers say."

"I remember. I also remember times when both Mama and Papa despaired because of your bullheadedness. Your tendency to barge on through something without thinking of consequences." Rebecca might be intrigued and wonder where this story was headed, but she wasn't about to let Colleen cover herself with stories of high praise when, at the same time, the girl could also tell tales of the trouble she'd gotten into often enough.

"Ah, consequences. That illogical action one takes following what seems like a very good idea at the time," Colleen said, still talking as if she dreamed.

This detachment should have scared Rebecca, but instead aroused her anger. "Get on with it. You did something, and now you've decided whatever that was wasn't such a good idea after all."

"You're so smart, did you know that, sister?"

"What is wrong with you, Colleen?"

"I suppose you can blame this on Lawrence Young."

"Lawrence? That boy you talked to all the time in the village? He and his father moved to California or somewhere on the west coast, didn't they? Some time ago, I think." Rebecca frowned, trying to remember the young man's face.

"Yes, that Lawrence. Beautiful blond hair and the greenest eyes. And muscles. Oh, yes."

Now Colleen was scaring Rebecca.

"What does this Lawrence have to do with you and what's going on now?"

"Well, you see," Colleen finally turned to look at her sister, "this is where the story really begins." She turned back to focus once more on the lake. "Lawrence worked at the paper. We used to talk all the time. We talked about a million things, like what it was like to be a man in this day and age. And what it was like to be a woman. We even talked about the human body. Oh, we also talked about courtship and marriage, but we both agreed we weren't interested in that."

A sickening thought entered Rebecca's mind and refused to lie down and die. She feared what she might hear.

"As fascinating as all these topics were, the idea of the human body must have stayed with both of us. I know I certainly dreamed about it...about Lawrence and what his body might look like. He even told me one day that he'd dreamed about me the night before and embarrassed himself in bed."

"Oh dear, Colleen, tell me you didn't."

"Oh yes, dear. We did."

Her dreaminess infuriated Rebecca, who marched right up to her sister, took her by the shoulders, and shook her as a terrier does a rat. "You stupid girl! What have you done?"

Colleen didn't react, instead continuing. "We explored

our bodies, together. He touched mine, and I touched his. When we finished touching, we explored more. I tell you, Rebecca, a man's body fits a woman's so perfectly."

"Oh, God!" Rebecca wanted to throw up, slap her sister, and scream all at the same time. "And how long did this go on?"

"Several months. We really had a lot to explore about each other, you see. So much bare skin, my breasts, his pecker. I tell you, sister, it was heaven."

"For God's sake, Colleen, are you with child?"

"Oh sister, I do believe I am. I felt it move today. Just like having a tiny Lawrence tucked below my heart."

Infuriated at her sister's casual dismissal of a problem that only time indeed would solve, Rebecca reared back a flat hand and slapped Colleen as hard as she could. The girl's head bounced off a rope and rattled Colleen so that she shook her head. "Why the devil did you do that?"

Even with a livid handprint across one side of her face, Colleen never shed a tear. Perhaps she still existed in that dream-like world she and Lawrence Young created.

"You stupid girl! What the hell were you thinking? You're smart. You've read books. You know what can happen if a man and woman lie together like that! And now you're bearing a child with no father. You told him, didn't you? That you were expecting his child."

Colleen nodded, even as one hand soothed her burning cheek.

"Of course he wasn't about to stay and father a child of his own carelessness. He probably went to his father for help, and the man packed them both up. They're long gone, and you're living in a dream world where things will be dandy. I watched Mama carry you and Hannah. She almost died with Hannah. That's why Mama's like she is."

"But I've not been sick one day, Rebecca." Colleen turned innocent eyes to her sister, eyes filled with tears that refused to fall.

"Well, lucky you! What do we do when you grow big without a husband to share this burden? What do we tell Mama? And Hannah! How do you explain to an eight-year-old that her sister laid with a boy and now carries his child, but the young man was too cowardly to live up to his obligations as a father so has disappeared into the wild west? What do you say to all that, Miss Colleen?"

As furious as Rebecca was, this news scared her to death. *What if Colleen dies while having this child? What do I tell my little sister and mother?*

"He called me *dearest*. Said I was a quick study."

"And how would he know you were a *quick study* unless he compared you to the others he's also lured with his muscles? Ever think of that, missy?"

"I uh...I uh..."

"Yeah, '*I uh...I uh*' is going to have a baby this winter, and '*I uh*' is going to have to give it away or raise it by yourself."

"But I like babies, Rebecca. I've helped Gloria and Jenny with their little ones. I helped care for Hannah, too."

"That's true. But you could walk away from those village babies when you were tired, and Mrs. Gordon, Hattie, and I helped with Hannah. It's just not the same as having one of your own, with only a few to help."

One would think Colleen would wake up and realize how wrong this was and how it was going to impact her life, but she didn't.

Rebecca turned her back on her sister so she could think.

"Another lie. You realize that, don't you? As long as we can, we must lie yet again. It's not safe to send you off to have this baby. Uncle Eugene would be all over us. And if he ever...when he finds out about this, he'll be on us for certain with no way back. You have to stay hidden as long as possible."

"What about Mama? Hattie? Mrs. Gordon?"

"Mrs. Gordon has had four children of her own. I'd be very surprised if she hasn't figured it out by now. Maybe even Hattie. Mrs. Gordon won't say a word to anyone. I'm not sure about Hattie...if she'll gossip in the village. We have no choice. You must stay close. I fear if you leave, you may never return."

"A logical decision at the time. An illogical outcome, I fear, now."

"That is more than enough truth for now. I can't take any more. You don't have more secrets you're hiding, do you?" Rebecca turned on Colleen with a nasty smirk.

"Really, you don't have to be so ghastly to me. I didn't think this would happen."

"But it did, and now we all must carry this around."

"Well, yes."

Rebecca rounded on Colleen once more. "'*Well, yes?*' What the hell kind of thing is that to say? Get to your room, and stay there until I calm down." She pointed a trembling hand to the house. "You better come up with a solution for this problem. Time takes care of the delivery, but time may not solve the ongoing problem of a baby where there should be none."

Colleen, ever one of independent spirit, lifted her chin and sauntered to the house as if she had not a care in the world.

"Oh sweet Jesus, help me now," Rebecca prayed as she sank to her knees.

The only answer she got was weather, as fragmented and chaotic as the mess Colleen dumped in her lap. The skies opened, and a summer storm broke loose, the likes they hadn't seen since the day of Robert Gilpin's death.

Chapter 16
Add One More

I *have to stop running, reacting to all that's happened, and take charge of this life we're living.*

Rebecca sat in the parlor, her sisters nearby. Hannah read while Colleen napped under a light lap throw. The half-opened windows allowed storm winds to blow in, but the porch kept the rain from entering. A wild night. A perfect match to Colleen's news that afternoon. Mama lay in bed upstairs. Hattie and Mrs. Gordon had to go home in the downpour.

Three more weeks. I can hold on that long. That letter satisfied Mama. Colleen... She rubbed her forehead after casting glances at the offending sister. *What do I do about Colleen? What if she wants to keep this baby? I can't let her go off...we have no relatives, nowhere to send her. We only have Uncle Eugene and his son. Uncle would delight in finding out about her condition. She would be on a train to somewhere on the west coast before we could gather our wits.*

Too restless to read or nap, she strolled around the room,

stopping by the window to let the wind blow away the cobwebs in her brain.

The only thing I can do now is brace up, as Papa often said, and start directing this ship. 'Trim your sails, young lady, and let the wind carry you to your destination. For sure, you won't be changing the wind.' True, Papa, but how?

The clock struck eight. Neither Hannah nor Colleen noticed the time. Only Rebecca did, struggling with how to keep the family together long enough to weather the storms that might descend upon them. *Might* being the key word.

She roamed the room, her mind bouncing like a rubber ball. She came up with ideas then discarded them. Nothing seemed advisable.

A noise intruded on her thoughts. At first she thought a shutter outside might have come loose and hit the side of the house in the high wind. Finally, she realized someone banged with a heavy fist against the front door.

"Colleen, wake up," Rebecca urged. She shook her sister where she lay napping. "Someone's at the front door, and I'm not opening it by myself in case it's someone intent on harming us."

"Huh? What?" Colleen struggled to wake, throwing off the lap rug, and slipping her feet off the sofa. Still half-awake, she joined Rebecca and Hannah.

"Who is there?" Rebecca kept a steady voice though her insides trembled, and her palms sweat against the fabric of her dress.

"Miles Jones from the village, Miss Gilpin. I brought a lady here that insists on seeing the family tonight. I couldn't persuade her to wait until morning. Says she has a train to catch at ten. I'm to wait."

"I know Mr. Jones," Hannah said. "Ask him what his

daughter calls her dolly." Hannah knew how to check out people.

"Mr. Jones, what does your daughter call her dolly?"

"Huh?" Suddenly a deep laugh broke out, overriding the noise of the storm. "Must be Miss Hannah asking. Victoria is what she calls that rag doll. Named after England's queen, she is."

Hannah nodded, and Rebecca threw the lock. Holding the door secure since the wind blew from that direction, she asked, "Who—"

Before she could finish her question, a small woman barreled past her into the foyer. Her arms carried something large. "I need to speak to the mistress of this house," the woman demanded in a voice loud enough to be heard over the storm.

Not sure if this woman meant them harm or not, Rebecca waved the buggy driver in. "Come in out of the weather, Mr. Jones. If you'll wait here—you may sit there— we will see what this woman wants. Miss...?"

The man thumped a carpetbag next to his feet but told Rebecca, "If it's all the same to you, miss, I'll wait in the buggy."

"If you wish, Mr. Jones, but it's very wild out."

"I think it best, miss."

"Very well." Rebecca shut the door behind the man but barely got turned around before the small woman holding the bundle sounded off at the top of her lungs.

"I'll be speaking to the mistress in private, thank you." The short, overweight woman carried herself as if she owned the world and all in it. She clutched the bundle despite the rain dripping off her travel cape and hat.

"The mistress is ill in bed," Rebecca explained. "I'm her

oldest daughter. These are my sisters. We will hear what you have to say in the parlor." Rebecca had no idea what was going on, but suspected privacy might be a good idea. "Hannah, perhaps it best if you—"

"I'm staying." Hannah seldom took a mule's attitude, but she did now. With no time to argue, Rebecca prayed she wouldn't regret allowing the child to stay. Turning back to the woman, she motioned her down the hall.

The woman seemed reluctant to move from the foyer, as if they might harm her. But she finally moved into the cozy room.

"Won't you sit? You look tired and hungry. Can we get you anything?"

"I'm needing only one thing. I came to deliver this young-gun'." Still standing, the woman held out the bundle wrapped in a colorful shawl.

"What?"

"This is your old man's son. My sweet Violet got kicked out of her wealthy home when Robert Gilpin got her with child. He paid for a room in a boarding house. Visited her every few weeks. Helped us out. I went with her. Her mother died of grief over the whole thing. Violet's father refused to have anything to do with her. Called her a harlot. Sweet Violet loved that scoundrel, though." She spit all that out in almost one breath.

As silence fell, the bundle moved. A hearty wail broke out from the damp wraps, around a sturdy body if the voice was any measure.

"Hush now, Davie," the woman cooed. "It'll be all right as soon as your family takes you."

"Wait! Wait!" Rebecca held out both hands palm out.

"Who the devil are you, and what right do you have to call my father a scoundrel?"

"My name is Patsy Roundhouse. I worked as a lady's maid to Miss Violet Chambers in Chicago. Miss Violet met Robert Gilpin at a function. They grew close, and finally Violet had to confess to her parents that she carried Gilpin's child. He's the only man my sweet girl ever met. She was mad about him. Truth to tell, I think he loved her too."

"Wait! Wait! This is all wrong. My Papa is happily married with three daughters."

"And now he has a son," Mrs. Roundhouse threw in loudly, her efforts to shush the noisy baby failing.

"Let me hold him. He may need a change." Fully awake now, Colleen reached for the child.

"Get that tote the driver brought in. All his things are in there. In fact, bring it back here. There's something in there that will convince Miss High and Mighty here that I'm telling the truth."

"Colleen, don't take that child! You have no idea if he's Papa's—"

"The child is upset, Rebecca. At least let me soothe him so he won't wake up Mama."

Reluctantly, Rebecca nodded. She turned back to the lady's maid, almost offering her a chair, but something perverse kept her silent.

"So why is this child here? I don't for a moment believe my father had anything to do with your mistress." She held up a hand to forestall the other woman's gasp. "I'm sure Violet Chambers was a lovely person, but my father..." She caught herself. She had almost said *was*. "Father would not do something like this."

Colleen returned with the still-fussy child and the tote.

She moved to the sofa, laid him down, unwrapped him and began going through the carpetbag with one hand while keeping the squirming infant pinned to the sofa with the other.

"While you're digging there, miss, find that photo frame."

Colleen dug through several layers of diapers and infant clothes until she came to the frame. She handed it over without looking at it and returned her attention to the child.

"Here, if you don't believe me. This is a photo taken shortly after Master David was born. That is Violet holding David, and that is Robert Gilpin with his arm around Violet, smiling at her."

Rebecca did not want to touch the photo frame even as she told herself that her father would never betray his wife or family in such a way. Reluctant or not, she held out her hand. The woman laid the frame in it then crossed her arms over her chest, waiting.

Slowly, Rebecca lifted the photo so she could look at it. Hannah nudged in beside her before Rebecca could move her aside.

"That's Papa!" A frown settled over Hannah's face. "Who's that?"

"That is Violet Chambers," said Mrs. Roundhouse. "Let me finish telling you the rest of the story."

Oh dear, another *story. As if Colleen's story this afternoon wasn't earth-shattering enough. As if this isn't worse.*

Before anyone could stop her, Patsy Roundhouse stuck her finger at the frame and finished the story. One Rebecca could never have imagined. By then, Colleen had soothed the child and moved up beside her sisters.

"That man moved Violet to a boarding house. He visited

and sent her money. I had a room in the attic. During her confinement, Violet's mother died. Grief, plain and simple. Mr. Chambers forbid the mistress from having any contact with her daughter. Broke the poor woman's heart, even though I sneaked around and visited when he was away. One day he caught me and threatened to call the law on me if I ever showed up again. Violet mourned something fierce, but Gilpin convinced her that she'd be all right. Not long before the baby's birth, Mr. Chambers died. Mugged on the way home from his club. He made no provisions in his will for her or her child. Never even mentioned them, though the lawyers knew he had a daughter. The will stated that all was to be sold and given to his club. A friend brought the news to Violet. She didn't mourn her father, let me tell you."

The woman stomped her foot. In anger or misery, Rebecca wasn't sure.

"Gilpin missed the birth of his son but showed up a week later. Time went on, and Violet grew stronger, just like the boy. One day Gilpin shows up, saying he's taking her to a fancy restaurant downtown. She came back with stars in her eyes. The next morning when he went out for work, she told me she loved him. Wanted to marry him. I asked her if he'd said anything about marriage, but she giggled and said he would. She just knew he would. That night Violet must have told him she loved him and would marry him if he asked."

The lady's maid stopped, took a deep breath, and put a hand over her mouth. Calmer, she finished. "The next morning, I had her tray and was coming down the hall to her room when I heard the most heartbreaking scream I never wish to hear again. I rushed to the door. But she'd locked it—or maybe never unlocked it for the day. The boarding house mister came and broke down the door. She sat on the floor, a letter clutched in her hand, rocking back and forth, moaning. Those moans like someone had killed her, but she hadn't died yet. I couldn't get her off the floor. I could barely get her to hush her moaning. She rocked like a mad woman. I pried the letter out of her hand and brought it too. But I never had time to read it until later, after..." She trailed off.

Like an automaton, she went to the carpet tote and rummaged until she brought out a letter. "Read this, and weep. For it killed my mistress as surely as if that man had stabbed her in the heart. She went out later that afternoon. To the lawyer, she said. She would attempt to get some of her father's finances for the boy."

She thrust the letter in Rebecca's hand and turned to face the window, one hand wiping tears from her cheeks.

Dearest Vi,

I do love you in my way, but I am married with three precious daughters. I cannot legally marry you without first breaking from those I have and love dearly. I will attempt to provide for David and you, but I cannot return. Your charm, grace, and beauty are too much of a temptation. And I am a weak fool.

With love,
Robert Gilpin

That broke Rebecca. She recognized the handwriting. Carefully, she folded the letter and put it in her pocket. "I assume the letter and photo are intended as proof of my father's weakness, as he put it?"

"Yes."

"Why is Miss Chambers giving up her son? Are there no other relatives?"

"There are no relatives, and Miss Chambers is dead!" The woman spit out the word *dead*, as if it tasted bitter. Her voice rose to what amounted to a scream. "She died of a broken heart. Threw herself into the river when she left me, saying she was off to visit her father's lawyer. *Robert Gilpin killed her* as surely as if he pushed her himself. And left a homeless babe. It's taken me three weeks to track down this man. That child—*that little boy*—is *your* responsibility now."

With that, the woman turned on her heel and made for the door. She threw it open, practically ran down the steps, and waved for poor Mr. Jones to open the buggy door. He jumped down from the high seat and got there in time to open it for her.

"Drive to the station. Make haste, or I'll miss my train!"

And just like that, the Gilpin house grew by one more.

Chapter 17
The Final Straw

"Robert?"

"Mama?" Horror filled Rebecca, and she set to trembling so badly she feared she'd not be able to walk.

"I heard Robert's name. What did she say? Killed?"

Rebecca, Hannah, and Colleen rushed to the foyer. Mama stood at the head of the stairs. Her skin matched the white of her nightgown, and her feet were bare. One hand held the handrail, but she looked none too steady standing on the top tread.

Rebecca feared something might happen to her mother. "Mama, stay where you are, and I'll come up and explain everything."

About that time, the baby let out a high-pitched wail. Colleen stood behind her sisters, attempting to shelter the child from view, but only a deaf person could miss his cries.

"Is that the baby? The one she talked about?"

Rebecca realized they'd not shut the parlor door in the chaos that Patsy Roundhouse created the minute she entered the house. Her mother must have heard most of the conversation.

"Mama, please, let me explain." Rebecca moved to the bottom of the staircase, but her mother dredged up unexpected strength and shouted, "Stop!"

So surprised was she that Rebecca stopped on command.

"Where is Robert?" Mama screamed. "That woman came because that's his child? Where is Robert?"

With no recourse, hoping that she could get to her mother before reaction set in, Rebecca hurried up the stairs as she finally told the truth. "He died, Mama. We hid the truth to keep us all safe from Uncle Eugene."

Rebecca reached for her mother, but Mama pushed her away hard enough that her oldest daughter stumbled back down several stairs, catching herself in time to stop from tumbling head over heels.

"He took a mistress? He had a child with that woman? He's dead?" Felicity screamed her rage, but as quickly as her anger flared, she went quiet. Her eyes rolled back in her head, her head tilted backwards while her body slumped forward. Like a loose rag doll, she fell down the stairs, hitting the balusters then the wall and back, her head thumping on each riser. It happened so quickly. Rebecca had no way of stopping her mother's fall.

Hannah screamed. Colleen screamed too, which set off the baby, wailing at the top of his lungs. Rebecca managed not to tumble down on top of her mother. But by the time she righted herself, Mama lay in a sprawled heap on the floor, her neck bent at an odd angle, one arm tucked under her and one leg wedged up against the wall.

"Colleen, take Hannah into the parlor."

When Colleen stood as if hypnotized by the tragedy in

front of her, Rebecca shook her arm. "Take the children into the parlor. Now! Hannah doesn't need to see this, and frankly, neither do you." Colleen's feet moved slowly, but her gaze remained on her mother's body. Hannah buried her face in her hands and sobbed with a broken heart.

"Go with Colleen and...David, dearest. I'll take care of Mama."

"She's dead too, isn't she, Rebecca?" Hannah spoke through her fingers without looking up.

"I'm afraid so, Hannah. But I'll check to make sure. Then..." At that moment, she feared their small group might repeat something similar to their father's burial.

And the storm outside raged on, eclipsed only by the chaos and fury that ensued inside the house.

"Go, girls. And close the door this time." She blamed herself that Mama heard the voices and came to check. To be honest, Rebecca had no idea how she would have, could have, explained a child in the house. She'd worry about that problem later. Right now, she wanted to check her mother.

Nothing indicated the woman still lived, but she did what Colleen had done with Papa. She felt under her neck for a heartbeat. Then she felt around on her wrist but wasn't sure she knew what she was looking for. Not finding what she searched for, she laid her head gently on Mama's chest. If her mother still lived, she'd hear the heartbeat. But no such sound came.

Sitting back on her heels, Rebecca sobbed. Hard and bitter the tears came. Her father's betrayal. A child thrown out because no one cared. Another child on the way. Now her mother dead at her feet all because Papa had chosen to do the unthinkable. Yes, Rebecca blamed her father for what had just happened.

Once again, the problems of the Gilpin household fell on her shoulders because this time there was literally no one else to carry the load. Colleen had her hands full. Hannah was too young, though the child had seen more of death in one summer than was good for anyone that age.

"Oh Mama, why couldn't you have gotten angry, stormed down here, and helped set this all to right?" She reached out to take her mother's hand but stopped. The neck and arm at such an odd angle. Torn fingernails where she hit the wall. An ankle with an unnatural bend. Gently, she moved hair away from Mama's face, but discovered her eyes open, the soft blue already clouding over in death. This wasn't her mother, any more than that man on the upstairs bedroom floor had been her father.

She stood, feeling like an old woman. Outside, the storm crashed on. "Why now?" she muttered to herself. "Why another storm? Can't we handle Mama without this?" Automatically, she turned out the gas light illuminating the foyer. The darkness would hide what no one wanted to see. But she wasn't leaving her mother uncovered like that. Down the hall she went and stepped into the parlor.

Both girls sat slumped, Hannah still with tears seeping down her face. Colleen held the baby to her shoulder, evidence she did know what to do with one. "I want that lap blanket, Colleen." She moved so Rebecca could get the blanket. "I need to go to Mr. Gordon's. Stay here. I won't be any longer than I need be. You must not leave this room. Please, I beg of you."

Hannah hung her head and nodded. Colleen gave her a distracted nod, the baby demanding attention.

Rather than throw the blanket over her mother, she laid it softly over her. Her mind going in a million directions, one thing surged to the front. Uncle Eugene could not find out about his sister's death for the few weeks remaining. Once Rebecca passed her birthday, the family would conduct a proper funeral. A private one, but notice would be given that Robert and Felicity Gilpin died of natural causes. On that matter, Rebecca knew Doctor Vincent should come and do what he did for Papa, complete with a paper stating Felicity Gilpin died of a fall.

Like Uncle Eugene will believe that. The immediate problem would be holding him off for another three weeks.

Bundled up in rain gear, Rebecca once more braved a storm to garner help taking care of her family. Only this time, she traveled alone.

Mrs. Gordon returned to the house with Rebecca so she could care for the baby that suddenly appeared in the household. Thomas went off to dig the grave, returning in time to meet Doctor Vincent who came in the Gilpin buggy with Mr. Gordon. While the girls and Mrs. Gordon waited in the parlor, the men took care of the body. When the three returned, they gathered the girls while Charlotte stayed with David.

"Mrs. Felicity is close by your papa," Mr. Gordon said with a sigh. He seemed more upset by her death than he was by Papa's. But then, he and Mama had often worked in the garden together. Mr. and Mrs. Gordon were there to welcome Robert and Felicity when they moved in, long before the girls came along.

Rain beat in fierce sheets against the sad group, making travel through the dark forest harder. This time, no thunder and lightning broke over their heads, but the rain intensified as the walk wore on.

Hannah struggled to keep up with Colleen and Rebecca.

She still cried, but did so quietly, which moved Rebecca to tears. Only Colleen seemed to take in the scene without a display of emotion.

As before, everyone returned to the house. Mrs. Gordon handed over the baby to Colleen and gave Rebecca a telling look. Doctor Vincent handed over a death certificate, saying Felicity Gilpin died of a fall, then joined Mr. Gordon outside. The gardener handed the doctor up into the buggy then drove off at a smart clip, the horse willing to move out if only to return that much faster to his dry stall.

"I'll stay the night, Miss Rebecca," Mrs. Gordon said. "I'll sleep in the parlor. You ladies shouldn't be alone tonight. Tomorrow will be time enough for plans."

"Thank you, Mrs. Gordon."

"Please, it's Charlotte, Miss Rebecca. You're head of the household now. It's only right."

With a nod, Rebecca assumed the rights and the duties.

Chapter 18
Explanations and Further Plans

Colleen slept little that night. David fussed. Finally, worn out and satisfied with a bottle of milk near dawn, they both slept. Rebecca knew because she remained awake. Hannah slept in Rebecca's bed.

Light filtered through gray clouds and a steady rain. Rebecca came into the kitchen before Charlotte. She opened the doors to the back porch and in toppled Thomas.

"What in the world? Thomas?" She helped him stand and dragged him into the kitchen. "What are you doing on the back porch? And in this terrible weather. You're drenched."

She hustled him to a chair, on the way relieving him of his jacket. "Let me get a towel so you can at least dry your hair and face. Take off those shoes, and set them by the fireplace. I'll start a fire in a minute."

By the time she hung up his coat on the back of another chair and rummaged through the downstairs linen closet, returning with a fluffy towel, Thomas had started a fire in the kitchen fireplace. "I wasn't sure how long you'd be, and I'm soaked through. Besides, you probably have more on your mind this morning than starting a fire."

She handed him the towel and pulled out another chair. Rubbing both hands over her face, she nodded, but remained silent for a few minutes while Thomas dried his hair and face.

"You're right. You know the situation. First Papa and now Mama. And Uncle Eugene looms on the horizon." She held up a hand, to keep Thomas from replying. "You've told me often enough what you think of our relatives. And I agree with you. But he can force me to wed if he learns no adult lives here. I find us in a distressing situation."

Charlotte entered the kitchen as Thomas and Rebecca sat in silence. "You! Thomas, what are you doing here? And soaking wet, I might add."

"I thought it best if someone watched outside...just in case. Mr. Gordon took the first watch for a few hours, but I relieved him early for my shift, knowing he drove to the village and back in this storm. He's at home, worn out."

Rebecca turned to give him a puzzled frown. "What did you expect to happen, Thomas?"

"I don't know. I just...I just thought it best if someone watched." He shrugged but didn't blush with embarrassment like she would have thought he might.

"I'm not sure what to say." She took his hand and gave it a squeeze. "Thank you. That was a kindness we probably don't deserve."

"Miss Rebecca, you ladies are in a tight spot now. Do you have a plan?" Thomas looked at Charlotte. "We'll help if we can."

"Again, a kindness we probably don't deserve. I've thought about what's happened. I'm hard put to ask anything of you without you knowing the full story. Yet I think the girls—well, Colleen at least—might object."

"Object to what?" Colleen entered the kitchen with David tucked in one arm as if she'd held a baby like that for years.

"You look so natural like that it's frightening," Rebecca commented.

"I told you, I've cared for the babies of a few friends, and I'm quite good at it."

"That may be the only blessing we have at the moment."

"So you said I might object to something. What is that?" Colleen set about looking around the kitchen. "Do we have any more milk, Mrs. Gordon? Or any more clean bottles? David used up the last one this morning."

She and Charlotte hustled around the kitchen, but Colleen repeated her earlier question. "Object?"

"Oh yes." Rebecca cleared her throat, gave Thomas an eye-rolling glance, letting him know that her sister could be a hound with a bone in such situations. "Things have gone to extremes, Colleen. With David suddenly showing up and you...well, you and your situation—"

"Her baby, you mean?" Charlotte asked in a voice smooth with innocence.

"Baby? More than one?" Unlike Charlotte Gordon, who knew the girls from infants, he apparently never noticed Colleen's widening waistline.

"Mrs. Gordon!" Colleen went three shades of red.

"Charlotte!" Rebecca jumped to her feet, not sure what she planned to do, but too stressed to sit any longer.

"What?" The housekeeper continued to rummage for baby things but turned an innocent expression to the head of the household.

Rebecca gave in and sat once again. "So that we might be safe until my birthday, I must explain to you two what's happened so that no one slips and says something that will alert Uncle Eugene or Cousin Ross to the reality of our situation." Rebecca turned to her sister. "That's what I thought you might object to. Knowing the truth is far better than assuming, Colleen. The Gordons—and yes, Thomas—must know what's going on. Thomas senses trouble already. Life must appear normal even with a baby just arrived and..." She swallowed, hesitated, but went on when Colleen cut her glance to Thomas then back and finally gave her sister a small nod. "And with you expecting a baby."

There! It's out now. No more tiptoeing around. No more wondering. That was the hardest part. Rebecca sat again and corrected her thinking. *No, that's not the hardest part. Explaining David will be harder.*

"I'm confused. Where did *that* baby come from?" Thomas jerked his thumb at David. He also asked the one question Rebecca—and probably Colleen as well—hoped he wouldn't. "And where's Colleen's husband?"

"Oh dear," Colleen said. By then, she and Mrs. Gordon had rounded up supplies for the baby. Colleen took a bottle of warmed milk, sat, and propped David on her lap. "You can explain better than me, sister."

Rebecca shook her head, rubbed sleepy eyes, and thanked God that Hannah still slept. Otherwise, the youngest sister would be down here asking questions before Rebecca could even begin her narrative.

With thumb and fingers massaging a growing headache over her brows, Rebecca turned to sit square to the table. She placed both hands on the tabletop, clasped them, and raised her eyes as if asking for divine help.

"Let me begin by saying that we often make decisions that seem logical at the time but later turn out to be quite illogical. There are consequences always, no matter good or bad decisions."

Those gathered nodded.

"First Papa. Well, no, let me back up even further. I have..." She really wasn't sure if she trusted them with this particular information but had no choice now. "I have helped Papa run the business for years. More than just as an accountant. I've signed papers with a signature so like Papa's that no one can tell the difference. In fact, by now, the contracts and documents for the last six or seven years are all signed by me. Papa taught me how to write, and we share the same initials. So assuming the reigns of the business in several months will be no problem.

"Papa came home that last night worried. I never found out what that was about, but knowing he had been in Chicago and returning unannounced several days earlier than expected, I can assume the reason. It seems..." She wiped her mouth as if a bad taste sat on her tongue.

This was hard. How to explain a parent's infidelity?

"It seems Papa found a mistress in Chicago, which explains some of the odd bills I've paid over the last year. Not only that, but that woman had a child." She held up a hand to ward off Charlotte's question. "I have proof. A photo of Papa, the woman, and the child. That child." She pointed to David, tucked into Colleen's arms, sleeping soundly. "There's also a letter—a distressing letter—that Papa wrote to the woman when..." She took a deep breath, because the rest of Papa's story showed him to be less than an honorable man. "Papa left the morning after the woman asked if he'd marry her. He wrote a letter to her, telling her he was married with three daughters. The young woman's parents had died, her mother shortly after learning about the coming child. Her father had cut her off completely, then died when someone tried to rob him. The young woman had no other relatives. She left the child in the care of the maid that came with her when sent from her home. Saying she was going to the lawyer's office, instead she drowned herself."

Charlotte and Thomas gasped. Charlotte laid a hand on Colleen's shoulder, perhaps to comfort.

Thomas rubbed his face and sighed. "Mr. Gilpin...I never knew him other than to see him in the house. This disturbs me that a man's actions led to an innocent's death. That's not...that's not..." He held his breath, begging Rebecca with his eyes to understand what he wanted to say but refused to.

"That's not honorable," she finished for him. "No, Thomas, it wasn't. He knew it even as he wrote the letter, then left. I think that's what worried him when I found him in the kitchen that night. Perhaps he wanted to take care of the woman and child. But that would have been financially consuming over the years and wouldn't have guaranteed she might not show up on the doorstep, anyway."

Thomas nodded, a look of relief on his face.

"In the meantime, Colleen told me yesterday that she and a young village boy had an affair. Not expecting anything to come of it, the young man and his father left the village for the west coast—location unknown—when Colleen informed him she was with child. Unlike Papa who apparently cared for his mistress and their child, this young man wasn't about to offer marriage. In that respect, I suppose he and Papa were the same. Less than honorable, both simply disappeared.

"So now we have a baby in the house. I suppose we can always say he is our ward, from a distant relative who died."

Rebecca rubbed her eyes once again. "No, that won't work. The Callaways know better. We have no relatives but them. Still, we can say we're adopting this homeless child. He *is* homeless, or was until he arrived on our doorstep. With proof that he is Papa's son, we can do nothing else. Papa's will says nothing about him. But we'll see that he's cared for properly.

"Now to Mama. When Patsy Roundhouse came in with the boy—thankfully, the driver returned to his buggy to wait for her—she wasn't shy about what happened to her lady, and she was adamant about us taking the baby. All of that at the top of her voice. We went into the parlor but forgot to shut the door tightly, such was the ruckus she created. As soon as she showed us proof of the boy's parentage, she ran out, entered the buggy, and drove off to the train station. Mama heard and came to the top of the stairs. But she was half asleep or something...she insisted on knowing what the woman wanted and why she insisted Papa killed her mistress. Rather than get mad, she simply fainted and pitched head over heels down the steps. You know the rest of the story."

If a mouse had scampered across the top of that kitchen table, no one would have noticed, so thick was the silence. So slack were the dropped jaws. So worried were the expressions that followed.

"That's the most incredible story I've ever heard," Charlotte said, sitting with a decided thump into a chair across from Rebecca. "Are you sure about all that? About Mr. Robert and a mistress?" She gave a quick sideways glance at the baby. "I'm not sure I believe that."

"I have the photo, Charlotte. I also have the letter. The penmanship is Papa's. I have no doubt. There are some odd financial transactions all from Chicago that now make sense, where before he actually got angry with me when I questioned them. I have no idea what I would have told Mama about the baby...if she'd lived. Perhaps it's a blessing she didn't. No! No," she said more calmly. "Mama's death—Papa's as well—was no blessing."

"But, Miss Rebecca," Thomas said, "her death means you have to lie to those scoundrels...your relatives, doesn't it?"

"I suppose you're right, Thomas. We must create yet another lie to save this family. But I'm not sure if we can put off Uncle Eugene long enough."

"We can say Mr. Robert is doing so well on the west coast that he'll be there another month," Charlotte offered, standing and pulling out items for breakfast. "And Mrs. Felicity is ill, and Doctor Vincent wants no visitors. She was weak already. Perhaps that might work. He and that boy of his don't come that often."

"That might work. Though Uncle and Cousin Ross have an uncanny knack of showing up at the worst times," Colleen added as she shifted David to her shoulder and patted his bottom. "Humm, someone needs a clean diaper. Let me know what you decide. At this point, I seem to be more of the problem than a solution."

Rebecca grunted in agreement rather than saying aloud anything considered mean. But silence didn't keep her from *thinking* mean things.

Chapter 19
Accepting the Way Things Will Be

T he household managed to survive two days of relative peace. Hattie arrived as usual to begin her day of cleaning and laundry. Immediately, she noticed baby things in the basket of dirty laundry.

"Oh, Hattie, we've had the most wonderful thing happen," Rebecca told her when she asked. "Mama agreed that we could adopt a baby, a homeless child. We got the little boy last night just after you left. His name is David." Rebecca didn't want to overplay the fact that a strange child suddenly appeared in the house. But she wanted the maid to accept the child with no hesitation. If Hattie did gossip in the village, the Gilpin family would look like heroes.

"He is a sweet little boy, Hattie." Colleen held the child in one arm, turned so Hattie could pat his cheek, drawing a smile from the six-month-old. One waving arm almost socked the maid in the nose when she bent forward to talk to the little boy.

"He's one we'll have to watch out for, miss. He has a strong arm there," Hattie teased.

"Too right," Colleen said. "Well, I'm off to the yard, so Master David can get some fresh air and not disturb Mama. She's taken quite ill, Hattie. Right after David showed up last night, we had to call for Doctor Vincent. Mama's not to be disturbed for any reason."

"I understand, miss. I'll be quite as a mouse."

"Thank you." Rebecca shooed Colleen down the long hall toward the back door, while Hattie went into the kitchen. "Be careful to stay close to the Gordon's house in case we have unexpected visitors." She walked Colleen out the door, then entered the kitchen door. "Charlotte, may I have some tea to take with me to the office?"

"Certainly, Miss Rebecca. Shall I prepare it and bring it in? Maybe a biscuit with it?"

"That would be lovely. Hannah is upstairs. She doesn't feel well."

"I understand. With her mama ill and all, the poor babe is feeling forgotten. I'll go up and check on her in a bit. Let her rest. Perhaps we can talk a little if she wants."

"Thank you. That might help her cope with the situation we now face. She must understand that silence is the key."

———

Rebecca saw the accounts in a new light now. Those numbers represented the future of her and her sisters. As well as David. The home and land, including the Gordon's home, belonged to the Gilpin family, so nothing to worry her there. Buyers showed interest in the jewels locked in the safe. The books reflected a healthy income with minimum outflow of cash.

"I suppose we won't have to worry about hotels, food, and travel now," Rebecca muttered. "However, sooner or later I must travel to several cities to deliver these jewels. How do I explain that Papa isn't available to come?"

She settled to work, going over the accounts, paying bills, and preparing mail—a typical day's work. However, before she left the office, she locked the photo and letter that Patsy Roundhouse had brought with David, along with the two death certificates, in the safe. She always carried the household keys. She'd done that since her Mama turned them over to her five years earlier. Yet another way of passing off her duties to a daughter not yet fifteen at the time. Now Rebecca secured the keys to Papa's office, the locked rolltop desk, her desk, and the safe to the ring.

————

"How are you doing, Hannah?" The little girl sat on the window cushion, her dolly cuddled in her arms, when Rebecca entered the room.

Hannah merely shrugged without looking around.

"May I sit with you?"

Hannah shrugged again but did move over several inches.

Rebecca squeezed into the space and leaned against the windowsill. Together they watched Mr. Gordon and Thomas trim the rose bushes. Now and then, Mr. Gordon would wipe his face as if a tear or two might have gathered. Colleen sat with the baby under the shade of an ancient oak, she and the child close enough for her to call on the men if needed. Rags ran between the two groups, his antics making the baby laugh. The three seemed to be visiting, while Rebecca and Hannah watched in silence.

"They are enjoying the day, dear heart. Why not join them? You and Molly Sue might be better for some fresh air."

A third shrug answered the suggestion.

"What is it, Hannah? What worries you?"

"You know."

"Mama?"

A nod and a sniffle.

"I wish with all my heart that had never happened. That Papa was home safe and alive. That Mama was well enough to help Mr. Gordon and Thomas in the garden and life was as it was a year ago."

"Not a year ago. That's when Henry died." Hannah pointed out important things in their lives, and the death of Rebecca's fiancé was important to the little girl.

Rebecca smoothed her little sister's hair and leaned on the palm of her hand. "Right you are. Perhaps we could wish for things to be as they were five months ago."

"Before Papa died."

"Yes, before."

"So why did he die, Rebecca? Why did he love someone else but not Mama? Why do we have a baby brother now?"

A deep sigh escaped Rebecca. Count on Hannah to ask the most important questions. "I can't give you answers to those questions, Hannah. Only God knows, and He's not saying. We simply don't know why people do what they do."

"Logical at the time, but illogical later. That's what you said."

"And whatever we decide to do—good or bad—always has consequences. That means something always happens because of what we do. Most often, it's wonderful, and we don't even think about it. But now and then those consequences turn out to be God-awful."

"So what do we do now?"

"First off, we accept David as our adopted brother, even though he really *is* our brother by birth. Can you do that?"

Hannah had to give that a lot of thought. "Will you still love me?"

"What?"

"I won't be the baby of the family. The *darling* that Papa called me."

"Oh, my dear, sweet Hannah. You won't be the baby because David will. But you will be loved so much until the day you die. And even after. You are loved this minute and the next and tomorrow and next Sunday and all the days after that." Rebecca gathered the little girl into her lap. "My, you are growing so much. No matter how big you get, young lady, we will always love you." She kissed the top of the little girl's head.

Hannah finally relaxed in her sister's arms. "So if we love David and he's our brother, then what do we do next? I know we are in trouble until your birthday."

"Oh, you are a smart puss, aren't you?" The compliment brought a smile to Hannah's face.

"Here's the plan. We avoid talking about David if Uncle Eugene and Cousin Ross show up. We avoid letting him talk to Colleen as well. She... Oh dear, this will be hard. Colleen did something foolish and is going to have a baby this winter. I'm not sure if the baby will stay or go to a new home, but there it is."

"Another baby? Will he be my brother, too?" Hannah wrinkled her nose.

"Well, let me think. Actually, this baby—we won't know if it's a girl or boy until it's born—will be your niece or nephew. Your sister's child. You'll be the auntie. That is, if the baby stays. Sometimes young ladies who have babies without marrying the father have to send their babies away and never see them again."

That got Hannah's attention. To Rebecca's surprise, her sister was angry. "How can I be an auntie if Colleen gives the baby away? No, we have to keep *that* baby, too."

"But who will look after David and the new baby?"

"Colleen will, and I'll help her." Hannah shifted her position onto the window cushion. "We can do this. A Gilpin problem. A Gilpin solution."

As much as Rebecca wanted to roll her eyes at the simplicity of Hannah's statement, she didn't. Hurting the child's feelings wasn't kind. "We're going to have to see what's happening when the baby is born in order to make a good decision. How about that?"

Hannah nodded, her attention back to the outside.

"Why not go out and play with David? He's young, but you can tickle him and talk to him. He smiled at Hattie this morning, so I'm sure he'll smile for you."

"Perhaps." Suddenly, Hannah didn't seem so sure about the little boy.

"You will be his big sister, you know. So you must take care of him, protect him, and make sure he's loved as much as you are."

"Perhaps," Hannah repeated. But she gathered her feet under her, scooted off the cushion, and straightened her skirt. "Come on, Molly Sue. You need to meet David. You're his big sister, too."

Like a general off to inspect her troops, Hannah marched out of the room and clomped down the back staircase.

———

"Dishes for you to wash, Hattie," Charlotte called as she came down the stair, carrying a tray. Each plate was empty, but Rebecca could tell each one once had food on it.

"How did you manage that?" she whispered.

"I pretended to take a tray up to Mrs. Felicity's room after I reminded Hattie that the missus was too ill to be disturbed. Then I carried tea and toast up there, ate it in the quiet of the room, and came back down after straightening the bed covers."

"I never thought about meals for Mama. That's brilliant, Charlotte."

"Thank you, Miss Rebecca. We have to keep this charade going another few weeks, then it makes no difference what that man and his son say or do. This family will be safe, and you can tell him where to go." The woman nodded her head emphatically but went silent when the maid appeared to take the tray. "Thank you, Hattie."

"Somehow *safe, Uncle,* and *Cousin* are words that just don't go well together."

"Amen, miss. Amen."

"Let us hope this peace and quiet continues."

"Like I said—amen."

Charlotte headed to the kitchen. Rebecca headed for the office. A buggy headed for the house.

Chapter 20
Shoulder to Shoulder

"Miss Rebecca!" Thomas flew into the office, his hair standing on end and his jacket askew. "The Callaways are headed down the drive!"

"Devil take them. What the hell do they want?" Rebecca offered no apologies for her crude language as she slammed the account book closed, stuffed it into the bottom drawer for the moment, and turned the key to lock it. Gathering her skirts, she breezed past Thomas, issuing orders as she ran down the hall.

"Take Hannah, Colleen, and the baby to the Gordon's house. Stay with them. If you see either of those two coming your way, take them out back and hide in the forest."

When Thomas hesitated, she shoved him. "Get going. Their safety depends on your fast feet. And send Mr. Gordon to the kitchen in case I need him."

"Right you are." He took off like a shot.

With the girls and baby safe and Mr. Gordon at her back if trouble came, she scampered into the kitchen. "Charlotte, Uncle and Cousin are almost here. Where's Hattie?"

"In the laundry."

Rebecca ran with her skirts hiked up to her knees around the corner of the house to the small area where the maid washed clothes before hanging them to dry. "Hattie! Hattie!" Thankfully, the maid knew how despicable the relatives were and often assisted the girls in not being alone with either man.

"Yes, miss? My goodness, what's wrong?" Hattie came out of the room with her sleeves rolled up and soap suds up to her elbows.

"Uncle Eugene and Cousin Ross are almost here. Please stay here. But if you must come in, say nothing about the baby. Uncle Eugene dislikes children. That would raise a lot of questions I don't care to answer right now."

"I'll just stay here, hidden from that younger man's roving eyes."

"Good girl. I'll let you know when they're gone."

She managed to be in the front foyer by the time the buggy stopped and both men approached the front door. She let them knock just to be perverse.

Opening the door, but not waving them in, she greeted them cordially enough. No sense in antagonizing them unnecessarily. "Good morning, Uncle. Cousin. I'd invite you in, but Mama's sick in bed and not to be disturbed. Doctor's orders, so we tiptoe around the house." Best to get the idea out there and see what they might do.

"May we come in and speak with you, Rebecca?"

"We can visit here, if that's all right with you, Uncle."

"I'm not as young as I used to be, and I'd appreciate sitting down with a cup of hot tea." He spoke in a civil tone that she had no argument against without raising suspicions.

She waved them inside and directed them to the drawing room rather than the parlor where Mama sometimes met them if she wasn't actually up to visiting but just being polite.

Charlotte appeared and stood silent at the doors.

"Tea please, Mrs. Gordon. Perhaps a cookie as well?"

"Yes, miss." The woman disappeared as silently as she had come.

"Is there something special I can perhaps help you with, Uncle?"

"Robert's still gone?"

Rebecca had to remind herself to keep anything she said short and simple. "He returned shortly, but only for two days. He made some wonderful contacts in California and took a train there as soon as he rested and packed a fresh suitcase. We really have no idea when he'll return."

"So he often comes and goes without staying long. Humm. Rather like a storm...blows in and just as quickly blows out."

Uncle is playing with me. I wonder what he wants?

"That happens sometimes."

"You say your mother is ill?"

"Yes, sir. We had Doctor Vincent out, and he gave her some medicine to help her breathe easier and rest better. But he forbids anyone but Mrs. Gordon and me going into her room. She gets excited easily and wants to come downstairs. She enjoys having meals with us and visiting in the garden with Mr. Gordon. But that's too much activity for her right now."

Lies. Lies and more lies.

To her surprise, Cousin Ross stood and moved to sit beside her. He took her hand before she could stop him. "I think my father might be forgiven if he steps up and sees his sister for a moment."

Uncle Eugene stood and moved to the door, heading down the hall.

Rebecca attempted to follow, cut him off, but Ross held her hand too tightly.

"Let go of me right this instant, or I will hurt you where it counts." She raised her other hand, a tight fist ready to land in the man's groin. Ross let go of her hand so quickly he fell backward on the sofa.

On the run now, Rebecca managed to slide in front of Uncle Eugene before he could step on the first riser. "That's far enough, Uncle. You will not endanger my mother's life by intruding on her privacy while she's ill." She stood eye-level to him.

The look of shock on his face quickly turned to anger. His brows went down, his eyes squinted, and his breath came hard from his nose, sounding like an angry bull preparing to charge.

"Young lady, I warn you. Move or—"

"Or what?" She stood her ground, terrified her uncle would push past her and make for her mother's room, if he even knew which one it was.

"Problem, Miss Rebecca?" Mrs. Gordon moved next to the newel post, her shoulder practically touching the stair rail. In her left hand, she held a cast iron frying pan.

"Did I hear shouting?" Mr. Gordon took up a position beside his wife.

With Rebecca standing on the second riser, Mrs. Gordon and her husband walling off the side of the stair-case, Uncle Eugene took a second to rethink his plan. Cousin Ross came up to stand behind his father but offered no support in moving up the stairs past Rebecca or her staff.

"Mr. Gordon, can you—?" Thomas entered the foyer and stopped beside Mr. Gordon. "Is everything all right?"

"Uncle, is everything all right?" Rebecca stood with her hands at her side, fists tight, ready to defend her family if necessary. She reasoned she'd never get a chance. Charlotte's frying pan would knock him unconscious, and everyone but Ross would swear that it was in Rebecca's defense.

"Uncle?"

"Very well. I won't bother my sister. How long has she been ill?"

Not fooled for a second, Rebecca didn't move from the center of the riser. "Several days. Doctor says she'll need bed rest for at least two weeks after the fever breaks, and she can sit up and eat a little." Despite the butterflies marching up her stomach into her throat, she tried to maintain a calm expression, not giving Uncle Eugene or Ross reason to think she was lying.

Lying comes so easily these days, she mused as Eugene took a step back. "Your staff seems concerned that there is a problem." He held both hands, palms out, at his side. "See? No problem here. Just concern for my sister's health."

"I think it's time you leave now."

That caught Eugene's attention, which was the last thing Rebecca wanted. She wanted him gone.

"*You think?* And who are you, *missy*, to tell me when I should leave? You're no one."

"When Papa is away and now that Mama's ill and can't have visitors, I am in charge of this home."

"Do tell. A bit high for yourself, aren't you, *missy*?" He sneered at her and eyed her up and down.

"Her word is good enough for us," Mr. Gordon said as he stood straighter and put one foot forward.

Charlotte raised the frying pan and thumped it softly against the newel post. "Good enough. Time's wasting, gentlemen. I have a meal to prepare."

Rather than argue, the Callaways picked up their hats from the foyer bench and left.

No one in the foyer moved a muscle until the buggy turned and headed back up the drive. Even then, Thomas moved to the sidelight and watched. "All clear."

"For now." With an unladylike thump, Rebecca collapsed onto her bottom on the stair riser. "I've never lied so much in my life. The pastor would be busy the rest of his life trying to save my soul—if he knew about all this. Which he never will." She rested her head in one hand, propped up on a knee.

Charlotte leaned against the newel post and let the pan sag. She relaxed so much the pan slipped out of her hand and landed with a decidedly loud clatter onto the floor, making them all jump.

"Jesus!" Charlotte slapped a hand to her chest, right over her heart. "That scared the stuffings out of me!"

"We are something, aren't we?" Rebecca stood and turned to the three with a grin that showed relief. "You three were wonderful. First one, then the other innocently showed up. But Charlotte, with that frying pan, was the turning point. The way Uncle looked when you thumped that post. I wanted to laugh aloud." Weak with relief, she did in fact giggle. "I'm not sure how soon those two might return." Seeing the skepticism on three faces, she assured them, "Oh, they will return. You all may not be around when they do, but I'm thinking a wall of determination beat them back this time. Thank you."

She made her way to the floor and hugged first Mrs. and Mr. Gordon then, after only a second's pause, hugged Thomas as well. "I couldn't ask for better friends. And now," she moved to the front door and threw the lock, "I think we can return to whatever we were doing before those two showed up."

The four parted, Thomas last. "Miss Colleen and little Miss Hannah are in a swivel, wanting to know what happened. Shall I bring them back? I'm sure Mr. Gordon will let me steady them on."

"Would you help them? That would be wonderful. You must tell them how bravely you and the Gordons stood up to the Callaways. That will delight Colleen."

"Off to fetch the young ladies, then." Thomas left, and Rebecca sagged onto the bench by the front door. She wiped the sweat off her forehead and sent up a prayer. "Father God, I'm lying for my family. I doubt that makes a difference in the Judgment Book, but it does down here. Forgive me, but I'm going to tell lies until this is over in a few weeks." Satisfied that she'd at least told the Lord how it would be, she went into the parlor, to wait for her sisters.

———

"Thomas said that he and the Gordons were in the hallway when Uncle Eugene tried to force his way upstairs," Colleen said over lunch. Colleen had relinquished David to Hattie. The baby had fallen asleep, and the maid volunteered to watch him while Colleen and her sisters ate.

"He never mentioned how they helped me back him down?" Rebecca sliced warmed roast that Charlotte managed to prepare after they had cleared the front hall.

"They what?" Hannah dropped her fork and knife onto her plate and turned an excited face to Rebecca. "Did they fight Uncle?" She raised her fists and shot them through the air as if she were boxing someone.

"Oh, for goodness sake. No, we didn't fight Uncle, though Cousin Ross held my hand so tightly that I did raise a fist and threaten to harm him if he didn't let go. He's such a weak person that he relinquished my hand immediately."

Colleen giggled, then broke into a laugh. "Don't tell me you threatened to hit him where it would hurt the most."

Rebecca nodded like a prim schoolteacher, and Colleen went off into a fit of laughter.

"What's she laughing about?" Poor Hannah wasn't old enough to understand how deeply a man protected his most private parts.

Afraid Colleen would come out with something too crude for Hannah to hear, Rebecca gave as simple an answer as she could muster without joining Colleen's laughter. "Uh, sister, a man has parts between his legs that help him when he marries and wants to get a woman with child. Please don't ask me more about it. Someday I will tell you so you will know what to do when the time comes. But suffice it to say, a man protects himself from injury there. I merely raised a fist and said I'd hurt him in those parts if necessary."

"Can I remember that now? I might need it for Jimmy Connelly if he ever bothers me again."

"Uh, Hannah, I don't think you need to worry about that at this time."

"But it's all right if I remember it. Just in case."

Colleen laughed so hard now, she had to lean against the table and hold her stomach.

"Very well, Hannah. You may remember it, but you will

ask me first before you use that knowledge. Do you understand, young lady?"

"Yes, I understand." Hannah lifted her fork and commenced eating, but had to have the last word. "I bet Jimmy would think twice about teasing me if I looked at that spot between his legs and raised a fist."

Chapter 21
Small Victory

Charlotte and Rebecca spent the next day straightening Felicity Gilpin's sitting room and bedroom. They kept the curtains drawn but opened the windows just enough to allow fresh air as would suit an invalid. Sheet and bedclothes went downstairs to Hattie in the laundry. Nothing unusual in that. Charlotte continued to take a tray up several times a day, sitting in a chair, napping after drinking the weak tea and eating the dry toast that Mama always enjoyed. Rebecca often took a book in there to read, sitting near Mama's bed. The day would appear normal to anyone asking. Hattie knew nothing other than the lady of the house was ill.

David thrived. Colleen had a knack for taking care of him, though Hannah and Rebecca played with him as well. On fine days, the three took the baby outside. Thomas often came over to tickle the little one and talk silly to him. Even Mr. Gordon stopped by and held the little boy.

"Miss seeing my grandson, I do," he often said. The

Gordons had two sons, but both lived out west. Only one had any children.

"Feel free to hold him anytime you feel the desire, sir." Colleen had mellowed with the passing of time, short as it had been since the revelation of her condition and Mama's death.

Rebecca felt that her sister might turn out to be an excellent mother after all. At times, Colleen still had tart remarks to make, but she'd learned to save those for necessary times rather than use them to hurt others.

"I can't believe the weather has been so mild for this late in summer." Mr. Gordon had been watering the flowers closest to the house, but several trips to the water barrel and back to the flowerbeds left him worn out. Thomas took over the duty while Mr. Gordon supervised. "That's one smart lad there, Miss Rebecca. Wish we could keep him. He reminds me of my youngest son, Benny."

"He returns to college soon, doesn't he?"

"Yes, but he plans on working somewhere close by when he finishes." Peter winked and gave a small nod toward Colleen. "Seems the boy's found something—or someone—interesting around here." With a chuckle, he went to help Thomas water the damask and maiden blush roses that grew closer to the wooded area.

"When David is old enough to walk, my child will still be an infant. But the two will be very close in age," Colleen observed as she moved into the chair Mr. Gordon vacated. She bounced the boy until he laughed, but then turned serious eyes on her sister. "We must record his proper name, Rebecca."

"I agree, but not until I'm twenty-one. Imagine what

Uncle Eugene would say if he learned we took in an orphan and then discovered in the natural way all snoops have that his sister and brother-in-law are dead, leaving three girls and a baby behind. Oh yes, I think it wiser to wait until the dust settles."

"I hadn't thought about the Callaways. Have you noticed how quiet Ross had been when he's visited the past several times?"

"Now there's something *I* hadn't paid attention to." Rebecca leaned an elbow against the arm of her chair and pondered that. "Is he attempting to look more desirable by not following in his father's boisterous way of managing things? Humm, surely neither of them is that smart. Papa told me on several occasions that rumors abounded about the Callaway wealth...or lack of."

"Really? No wonder they pursue you...and this house. With Mama tucked under their feathers, those two yard birds could rule the house if they ever found out Papa was...well, if Papa had no more say in matters."

"And I would be married to Ross in nothing flat. We face the same situation we did when Papa died. Keeping the relatives at bay for a little longer."

———

Twice more, those relatives came to the Gilpin home. Rebecca never met the two in the parlor. That was now reserved for family only, as far as she was concerned. She directed them to the more formal drawing room.

First Uncle Eugene came in, more decorous than the previous time. He visited with Rebecca for less than fifteen minutes, inquiring about his sister and brother-in-law.

"Mama is over the worst, but still so excitable. Doctor

Vincent thinks the medicine that has eased her illness also sets her off. The best thing, he says, is to keep her as calm as possible, or we could cause a setback." She nodded solemnly, while Eugene had the decency to look worried.

"What about your father?"

"He has buyers lined up for the items he found on the west coast. He traveled up to Seattle and ventured to Vancouver while there. He has found some great treasures." Rebecca managed to tell Eugene this without telling him that her father dealt in rare and unusual jewels. The man would positively salivate if he thought that much money was coming into the family.

Eugene departed, none the wiser for what his sister's husband did for a living.

Next came Ross one cloudy day. He brought flowers that Hattie put into a vase and returned to the drawing room.

"Rebecca, you look tired. Do you have a nurse to take care of Aunt Felicity?" He sat across the small table from her. His voice carried a warm and caring tone that she thought too solicitous when compared to how he acted in the past.

"I'm well, thank you. I had a late night, finishing a good book." She knew he seldom read. He'd said as much over the years. She never remembered discussing books with him.

However, those who are desperate to make a good impression often do foolish things. Ross crossed one leg over a knee, sipped his coffee, and asked, "And what are you reading, pray tell?"

"A delightful book about a group of sisters and their mother during the Civil War. You may have heard of it, *Little Women*, by Louisa May Alcott. I find the family in the novel similar to my own family. Have you never read anything that reminds you of your family?"

Ross lifted his eyes as if trying to remember anything he'd read that answered that question. "Uh, no, cousin. I don't think I ever have."

"I love reading. The words take me away to distant lands and strange adventures." She gushed over the subject, thinking he might change to a new topic.

Instead, Ross set down his cup and saucer, snapped up a cookie and stood. "I think the family must be doing well, having such time to flitter away at reading. I'll take myself off then."

"I'll see you out, cousin."

They moved to the front foyer where Ross picked up his hat and leaned toward Rebecca, as if to kiss her cheek. Again, she stepped back, a frown replacing the pleasant smile she wore seconds earlier.

"Really, cousin, I simply want to kiss your cheek as one relative does another." Ross acted as if she'd hurt his feelings deeply.

"I don't care to be touched in such ways. I'm asking you not to do that again. Men do get slapped on occasion for taking such liberties, you know."

"Liberties? Slapped! You go too far, Rebecca." With that, he crushed the cookie and let the crumbs fall to the floor tiles. One big step and he stood on the porch. He pulled his hat onto his head hard enough to crush it down around his ears. Not realizing he looked silly with his ears pressed flat, he saw the twinkle of humor in his cousin's eyes and took exception to it. "You will regret such words, missy."

"Now you're just being silly, and worse, you and that *missy* sound like Uncle Eugene. Goodbye, Ross. If you happen to come again, and I really hope you don't, please bring your good manners. They are *so* important, you know."

Her sweet demeaning words infuriated Ross, but short of storming the front door and risking a possible run-in with the law, he stomped to his buggy and startled the poor horse into an immediate run by whipping it mercilessly.

———

"Good news. Bad news," Rebecca said when she went upstairs after Ross's buggy cleared the drive. Colleen and Hannah sat playing a game of cards. David slept in a baby bed that was once Hannah's. Papa had stored it in the attic years before. "Which do you want first?"

"Good news!" Hannah beat Colleen in laying down her card only because the middle sister was looking for a good card herself.

"Bad news please." Colleen slapped down a card, crowed about winning the hand, and insisted Rebecca deliver the bad first. "Only makes sense, Hannah. We groan over the bad and cheer over the good. Makes me feel better to laugh rather than leave the room crying."

"I suppose you're right. The bad news please," Hannah conceded as she gathered the cards for the next hand.

"Cousin Ross just left."

"That's bad? I don't think so," Colleen sneered.

"Oh, that was probably the good. Sorry. No, the bad part is that I angered him, and while I hope he never returns, I fear he and Uncle will come back with a vengeance, demanding to see Mama. Demanding she discipline me for my treatment of poor Ross." She lifted her eyes and patted her heart with both hands, imitating her cousin in a girly type of way.

"Oh, now that is bad. So what made him so mad that you think they might seek revenge?" Colleen laid the cards to one side; she was to deal next. The game lost its interest in light of the real-life game the family played with the two Callaway men.

"I suppose this is part of the good—him leaving. I was tired of him about a minute after he entered the house."

"So what happened?" Hannah sat like a bird eyeing a worm, excited and ready to pounce.

"First, he accused me of looking tired."

"Well, frankly you do."

"Thank you so much for that support, Colleen." Rebecca dragged out her sarcasm, forgetting that her sister usually had a witty, if sarcastic, comeback of her own.

"You're most welcome, sister."

Rebecca growled but chose to ignore Colleen. "I told him I'd been reading all night—a delightful book."

"Well, that should have killed the subject. I've never seen Ross with a piece of paper in his hand much less a book." Colleen leaned against the side of her chair with a knowing look. "That didn't stop him, did it?"

"No. You could have knocked me sideways with a finger when he asked what I was reading. Thankfully I just finished *Little Women*—"

"I love that book!" Hannah clapped. "That isn't something a man would read, though. I bet he's never heard of it."

"I think not. I told him it was about sisters and their mother during the war and all the things they did. How it reminded me of my family."

"Ooh, I bet that made him want to go out to the lending library and get a copy." Colleen arched her brows and spoke in mocking tones.

"I doubt it, sister. But I went on and on about reading. He jumped up and said it was time to leave. That the family must be all right since we have such time to flitter away reading."

"*Flitter*? I had no idea the man knew such big words."

"That's an awful thing to say, Colleen."

"But oh, so true."

The girls spent a few moments laughing softly so as not to wake the baby.

"That's not made him angry, though."

"There's more?"

"I escorted him to the door where he proceeded to crumble a cookie on the floor like a child, after he tried to kiss me."

"Oh." Both Colleen and Hannah wrinkled their noses.

"He's tried it before. The first time, I backed away and gave him a nasty look. This time I did the same and told him I don't want to be touched, and certainly not kissed, by him. I told him if he ever tried it again that I would slap him."

"You didn't!"

"I did!"

Colleen applauded. "Well done, sister!"

"That's when he crumbled the cookie. Then he stepped on to the porch and..." Rebecca had to stop for a moment as the memory of how silly Ross looked flashed through her mind. "That's when he pulled his hat down so hard because he was so angry that his ears stuck out flat. He looked so silly that I almost laughed, and he knew it. When he left, he was spitting mad."

"I wish I could have seen that." Hannah leaned against her hand, her card game forgotten. "He's not very nice. To me, to Colleen, or anyone. I wish I could have laughed at him. That would have served him right."

"That is good news," Colleen agreed. "He left looking

silly, knowing he's not welcomed. As Hannah said, that serves him right."

"All that may be true, sisters, but one thing we can't forget. Ross is like Uncle Eugene. Cunning. And I daresay, mean when embarrassed. I embarrassed him badly just now. He will want his pound of flesh in return." Rebecca took the empty seat at the small table. "As much as I hate to say it, I enjoyed the moment and the retelling, but now I wonder if I really won the war. We may have a victory here with both men off in a huff and not likely to bother us again. But—"

"Look, gloomy puss. You won. Take that victory and celebrate." Colleen was up for some fun, apparently. "Let's get Mrs. Gordon to cook a special meal, then invite the Gordons and Thomas, and we all celebrate putting down Cousin Ross. We don't have to tell the others the details, just that you got the best of him, and it's time to have some fun. Maybe Mr. Gordon has some fireworks in the storage shed. Wouldn't that be fun?"

"You know what? I think you're right. I told myself last week that I needed to take control of our lives and keep us together. Perhaps I did just that today when I forced Ross to back off. Between embarrassment and Charlotte's frying pan, neither will want to come back any time soon." One hand out to each sister, Rebecca gave them the first genuine smile she'd enjoyed in several weeks. "Let's celebrate a long-awaited victory."

Chapter 22
A Small Celebration

Off Thomas went to the village butcher for a special cut of roast. Rebecca and Hannah gathered summer vegetables. Colleen and David helped Hattie gather fresh peaches so Charlotte could make a pie.

"Hattie, won't you join the family in a special dinner this evening? We just feel like celebrating, what with Uncle Eugene and Cousin Ross off for a while," Rebecca asked as she laid down her armload of carrots.

"Oh miss, that's lovely of you for asking me, but Mr. Johnson expects me home for our own evening meal."

"Perhaps another time. Maybe for my birthday."

"Now that would be a grand occasion." Hattie accepted the fruit Colleen carried in one arm while she carried David in the other. "Mrs. Gordon, I can't stay for the fun tonight, but I'd like to help prepare the meal or whatever you need while I'm here."

"That's nice of you to offer, Hattie. Perhaps you might

help set the table outside after Mr. Gordon and Thomas get the tent set up.

"Thank you, Hattie," Rebecca added.

Meanwhile, outside on the green lawn always kept clipped by Mr. Gordon, he and Thomas set up a white summer tent, open on each side. The tent would shade the family while they ate but would allow breezes to come through. Once they moved a large board to the spot and supported it on sawhorses, Hattie helped them bring chairs off the front and back porches as well as the Gordon home. Then she threw a sparkling white cloth over the board and proceeded to set the table for the evening meal.

Mr. Gordon whispered to Thomas, who immediately set off with clippers in hand. When the younger man returned, he held armloads of cut flowers. Hattie clapped her hands and went to find vases. By late afternoon, smells coming from the kitchen set the mouth to watering. The table gleamed with shining glasses, plates, and vases of flowers.

The girls spent the afternoon in the kitchen with Charlotte, David in a swinging crib brought down from the attic. His kicking feet kept the crib moving enough to entertain him. He gurgled and cooed enough to entertain the ladies. Thomas and Mr. Gordon came in now and then to see if they needed anything.

Rebecca thanked Hattie and sent her home early. That way, no one had to explain Mama's absence. Hattie might have heard Rebecca telling Eugene that his sister was improving.

Finally, the roast sat on a giant platter, resting in its own juices. Bowls of vegetables sat nearby. Two pies sat cooling in the pie safe. Hannah and Rebecca carried pitchers of water out. Colleen carried David while Thomas carried the swinging crib. She filled water glasses with the baby nearby. At last, Mr. Gordon and Charlotte carried out the meat, with Rebecca and Colleen carrying the bowls. Hannah brought a tray of warm bread and soft butter.

When all sat, with Rebecca at the head of the table, the sun still shined but was near the tops of the trees across the lake. Peter and Thomas had lit lanterns earlier just in case the meal went until after dark.

Rebecca stood and held her glass. "This is an amazingly beautiful moment. Friends and family gathered to celebrate... well, a number of things. Summer ending soon. Our closeness, the last we hope to see of Uncle and Cousin." Those around the table laughed and held up their glasses. "I toast the best we have to give and have given." She raised her glass and sipped, as did the others.

Oddly enough, Colleen stood as her sister returned to her seat. "I want to offer one last toast before we enjoy a meal that is hot now. So I won't say much lest it all get cold." The others again laughed, but sobered slowly when they saw that she wasn't in a jesting mood. "This year has brought the most unexpected things to our home. Tragedy. Anxiety. And perhaps a bit of hope." She paused to touch her rounding stomach. "Lest we forget. We should toast those who are gone but never forgotten. To Robert and Felicity Gilpin."

Each one at the table stood, lifted glasses, and repeated, "To Robert and Felicity Gilpin." When they sat, no one moved or spoke.

Naturally, Colleen, having started the sad mood, remedied it immediately. "I'm not sure either Papa or Mama would forgive us for missing this meal when it's hot, no matter how much we might miss them. Let us enjoy this scrumptious meal together as family."

They ate until each one leaned back, patting stomachs overfull with good food.

"I think you outdid yourself, my dear," Mr. Gordon said, leaning over and kissing his wife's cheek.

"Here! Here!" Thomas shouted and thumped the table.

The others joined him. The noise woke David who squirmed and began crying.

"Oops." Thomas beat Colleen to the crib. "Sorry, little man." He handed the baby off to Colleen.

"I'll get his bottle and change him. Be right back."

"I'll walk with you...just in case," Thomas offered.

"Just in case what?" Colleen and Thomas were already walking off, so no one at the table heard his reply.

Mr. Gordon winked at Rebecca who sat smiling while looking after the two. "See what I'm talking about, miss?"

"I do indeed, sir."

"Now, Peter Gordon, don't start making wedding plans for those two. You know how you are." Charlotte leaned over to Rebecca. "He no sooner found out our sons were marrying than he started making plans for the wedding. Like a man can do any of that."

Hannah sat listening, her focus on first Peter, then his wife, and finally Rebecca. "Will Thomas marry Colleen?"

"I have no idea, sweetheart, but let's not mention it to them. That might embarrass them, and we wouldn't want that, would we."

"Colleen would yell at me, and I don't want to hurt Thomas' feelings." She bounced up off her chair shortly after that particular conversation when she saw the two returning. "Mr. Gordon, can we get out the fireworks now?" The sun had gone down while they ate, and the sky was clear with a thousand twinkling stars.

"I think this is a perfect time. I'm getting old and need my rest, you know, so let's get those firecrackers out and have a booming good time."

With Thomas and Hannah helping, Mr. Gordon set up several rounds of fireworks. They wouldn't last long, but the colors, noise, and reason were all the family needed to have a good time.

"Ready to light up some?" Thomas stationed himself halfway between the ladies and Mr. Gordon. The girls and Charlotte had moved closer to the lake. "Colleen, lean David against your shoulder so his ear is covered, then use your hand to cover the other. The noise might scare him."

"Oh! Good idea!" she called. "Thank you."

"Wonder where he learned that?" Charlotte whispered to Rebecca.

"We may never know."

At that moment, the first of several strings of firecrackers went off. The flames, small as they were, went in the lake. The calm waters reflected the colored lights. Small firecrackers went off, then a few larger ones that Thomas called boomers. Those were the only ones that made David jump. His eyes, though, took in the colors and movement, and he never cried.

At last, the fireworks ended. Thomas extinguished the torch used to light them. Everyone returned to the tent. To a table filled with leftovers and dirty dishes.

"Oh dear, first the fun and now the work." Charlotte sighed. "There's always a price to pay, isn't there, miss?" Neither she nor Rebecca seemed to think anything long lasting might come of the comment.

"I'll tell you what." Rebecca picked up her plate, laid her

silverware and napkin on it and took up her glass. "Everyone take up their place setting, and let's take that to the kitchen. Then we return for the leftover food. Everyone carries something. Colleen is excused to carry one handful."

"Why thank you, sister. I honestly wondered if David might have to carry something, too."

"When he's older."

Colleen rolled her eyes but accepted Rebecca's suggestion.

Everyone marched back to the house, carrying their place setting. Like a well-oiled machine, each person moved to the sink, cleared up their mess, and put the glasses to one side so as not to break any.

"Now for the second round." Rebecca directed her companions outside once again, and they returned carrying the remains of the meal. "Now everyone carries their chair. Thomas may carry his and Colleen's."

Charlotte grinned, but only Rebecca could see her. "Matchmaking, are we?"

"No, just being practical. He probably would have done so anyway. This way Colleen won't tell him no and try to carry it and the baby at the same time."

"Yeah, I think you're right," Charlotte said, but Rebecca could tell she still thought the girl was putting Thomas in Colleen's way.

In less than fifteen minutes, the dishes and food were inside. The chairs sat on the back porch and the board and sawhorses were back in the shed, while the tablecloth and napkins went into the laundry room.

Before the group broke up, they hugged. No one was left out. The Gordons and Thomas left, waving and calling good night. The girls went inside, locked up, and went upstairs. Colleen carried a bottle of milk just in case David got hungry in the night. Recently, the little boy slept through the night, though he still preferred to wake up early.

"That was so much fun," Hannah said as Rebecca helped her into a nightgown. She yawned as her sister plumped pillows and pulled down the sheet.

"We certainly had a good time, didn't we? Now it's time for bed. I think we'll all sleep well tonight. Say your prayers, then hop into bed."

Hannah yawned through her lengthy prayers, but finally finished and dragged into bed.

"Sleep well, sweetheart. Love you." Rebecca pulled the sheet over Hannah, leaned over, and gave her a kiss on the forehead.

"Love you too, Rebecca. Night."

By the time Rebecca turned down the gas light and closed the door to Hannah's room, the little girl lay snoring ever so softly.

"You still awake, Colleen?" she whispered into Colleen's room.

"Not for much longer, I can tell you. I had a lovely time, but David and I are worn out. I don't think I've moved that much in a long time. All that coming and going." Colleen sat snuggled beneath her sheet and a light blanket. David slept in his crib not five feet away. "I doubt I'll turn over all night. Well, unless he gets to wiggling and fussing."

"He is a good boy, isn't he?" Rebecca smoothed the sheet on which the baby laid, his body covered only by his night sack. "Babies give off so much heat. No wonder he doesn't like a blanket on him."

"He's a regular firebox at times, but he's healthy. Still, I think it's time for Doctor Vincent to check him, just to be sure we haven't missed anything. And the doctor really needs to be aware of David's situation." Colleen fluffed the covers over her legs but avoided Rebecca's gaze. "And I think he needs to know…well, about me, too."

"Must he?"

"Sister, I'm having a child. I don't want the man to show up the day this baby is born and wonder what he might have missed all this time."

"When you put it that way, I suppose you're right. We'll send for him tomorrow. We can say he's coming to check on Mama, just to ward off any suspicions Hattie might get."

"Good idea. Thank you for saying we can have him out. That makes my day complete. Love you."

Rebecca turned off the gas light in her sister's room and closed the door. With a lonely sigh, she stopped by Papa's room, opening the door, but seeing nothing that reminded her of the man himself. The room looked like a guest room. His personal things lay in drawers.

Mama's room looked more as it did when she lived. Flowers stood in a vase at the window, visible from outside. But the bed was made, and the room lay in order. Not exactly how Mama had kept her rooms. She loved a bit of clutter here and there. Nothing much in that room reminded Rebecca of her mother, either.

Making her way to her room, Rebecca went through her nightly routine. Cleaning her face. Changing clothes. Tidying up the room. Unlike her mother, she could stand clutter for only so long before she picked up and put away. Normally she did that each evening, knowing her room would look lovely when she opened her eyes the next morning.

A sigh or two passed from her before her eyes closed in longed-for rest. Perhaps she had won the battle with her relatives after all. That thought eased her mind and sent her right off to sleep.

Chapter 23
The Day Arrives!

The following week remained calm, but hotter. Everyone slowed down. Doctor Vincent came to see Mama, or so Rebecca said. All but Hattie knew better. Upstairs the doctor went, trailed by the girls. Rebecca motioned Charlotte to follow. She wanted someone who had experience with babies and childbirth to listen to Doctor Vincent. Charlotte would know what was important where the girls would not.

"I'm not here for your mother or father." The doctor spoke softly. All the windows stood open. The family didn't want others like Hattie to hear, but the household had to look normal. "So who is in need of medical advice?"

All four ladies stood silent, not sure what to say. David cried as if on cue, and Doctor Vincent turned around to see the baby. "And who is this chap?" He moved to stand beside the bed, waiting for one of the ladies to speak.

"Uh, Doctor, this is David. David Gilpin," Rebecca finally said.

"Gilpin? A relative?" The doctor delivered all three girls

and knew Felicity could have no more children. "Surely not your uncle?" He frowned. He knew Eugene and didn't really approve of him. He'd told Rebecca that when she warned him, the uncle might make a play for moving in and taking over if he knew Robert Gilpin was dead. She reminded him of that fact when Felicity died.

"Uh, no. Not Uncle's."

Colleen pushed Rebecca forward, then returned to stand by Charlotte and Hannah, each with their hands in their pockets, silent as stones.

"Oh, bother." Rebecca slapped Colleen's hand away. She stuck her own hands in her skirt pockets and eyed the far window as she blurted out. "Father had an affair, and David is the result. He's about three months, we understand. The baby's mother is dead, and her lady's maid brought the boy here, expecting to tell Mama and make her take the child and punish Papa." She waited for the doctor to comment, but he said not a word.

Instead, he turned to the little boy, speaking to him softly. He lifted the diaper and gown, checking first this, then that. He hefted the baby into his arms and took him to the bed where he opened his bag and pulled out a scale and large cloth.

The cook and the girls watched, fascinated, as Doctor Vincent slipped David into the cloth triangle, then attached the ends of the cloth to the scale. Raising the whole contraption, he weighed the baby. "Right where he should be." After a thorough examination, he returned the child to the crib and turned to the ladies.

"I assume you plan to adopt the child."

"We will say that he was homeless—which he was—and we will give him a home and name. He will be David Gilpin."

"I can't say I'm not worried that a houseful of young ladies is alone to handle a baby. But Charlotte is here and can offer advice and help if needed."

Nodding like a mad woman, Charlotte agreed quickly.

"Good. Good. The boy is sound. I suggest you get him registered with a birth certificate and proper name as soon as possible." He gathered his instruments and closed his bag.

"Uh—"

"There's another problem that I can help with?"

"Well, two actually. Can we wait to register David for adoption with a proper name until after my twenty-first birthday?" Rebecca squirmed, realized what she was doing, and stopped. But she worried the man's scruples might not allow him to go along with yet another scheme. Two deaths may have been all right, but this was a baby.

"Worried about that uncle?"

"Yes, sir. He may accidentally find out about...well, you know. And he would swoop down on us faster than you can blink an eye. We'd all be tossed to the wind."

"And Rebecca would have to marry nasty Ross," Hannah added.

"I gather you and Cousin Ross aren't in love."

Colleen snorted. "That's an understatement if I ever heard one. They aren't even in *like*. Ross and Uncle only want their hands on the Gilpin money."

Doctor Vincent snorted this time. "Nasty pieces of work, those two. I've sat in the pub with your father a few times and heard his opinion of his brother-in-law and that man's son. Not complimentary, I can assure you."

"We're aware of that. But can we count on your discretion until such time as all can be out in the open?" Rebecca twisted her hands and broke into a sweat, her anxiety was so great.

"This is wrong, you know."

"Yes, sir, it is...I think. Maybe not. But this child and my family will be wronged...destroyed...if Uncle Eugene finds out about...Papa's indiscretion. Not to mention his and Mama's deaths."

"I agree. So your secret...secrets...are safe with me. Now, if there's nothing else." He moved toward the door, but Colleen moved into his path.

"Yes, Miss Colleen. You need something? Are you ill?"

"Yes, sir, I do need something, but no, sir, I'm not ill."

Puzzled by her reply, he stopped and gave the group another going-over. "So what can I help you with, miss?"

Rather than speak aloud, Colleen stood on tiptoes and whispered in the doctor's ear.

The man took a step back, gave Colleen a hard glare and cleared his throat, in the manner of a person not sure what to say. "I think Miss Colleen and I need to be alone for a few minutes. On second thought, Mrs. Gordon, would you stay with us, please?"

"Certainly, Doctor." The woman never moved but crossed her hands in front of her.

"Miss Rebecca, will you take Miss Hannah and walk out by my buggy while I finish here?"

"Yes, sir." Rebecca took Hannah's hand and left.

Downstairs, Hannah finally asked Rebecca why they had to leave. "Doctor Vincent wants to make sure Colleen and her baby are going to be all right."

"But the baby is inside of her."

"Yes, dear, but the doctor can listen and feel on the outside." Rebecca sent up a fast prayer asking that Hannah not ask any more questions because she had no way of making an eight-year-old understand being with child or preparing for childbirth.

I have no idea, Rebecca thought frantically. *How can I explain what I don't know?*

Not long after they got to the yard and stood petting the horse, Doctor Vincent came out of the house. Charlotte followed.

"Where's Colleen? Is she all right?" Her imagination running wild, Rebecca sounded a little desperate even to herself.

"Colleen is fine. The baby needed changing, that's all." The doctor climbed into his buggy and picked up the reins. "Mrs. Gordon, perhaps Miss Hannah might enjoy one of your ginger cookies. I smelled them as I came downstairs."

"Certainly, Doctor." Charlotte held out her hand to Hannah who was reluctant to leave.

"You're going to tell Rebecca something about my sister, aren't you?" She stuck her chin out and demanded an answer. Everyone could tell she wasn't leaving without one.

"Yes, I am, but all is well. So you can enjoy your cookie, knowing your sister is fine."

"Well, all right then." Just like that, Hannah marched off to the house, Charlotte trotting to keep up.

Rebecca joined the doctor in a gentle laugh. "Colleen really is all right? The babe she carries?"

"As far as I can tell, the child will be born around Christmas. Colleen is definitely in good health. She said she was never sick to her stomach, which is unusual, but we'll count ourselves lucky there. The baby moved when I felt Colleen's stomach. Unless she begins to bleed or hurts, I think she'll make it to the birth well enough. I'll check on her often though, just to make sure. I gather there's no father around?"

"The father of her baby left with his father shortly after he found out Colleen was carrying. He's not part of this family's plans going into the future. I'm not sure what we'll do about Colleen's baby—keep it or give it to another family. We have no family left but the Callaways. Colleen seems to be a good mother if you judge by how well she's handled David so far." Rebecca shrugged. "We just don't know about the coming baby. But David will stay. He's a Gilpin by birth. And yes, I have proof of Papa's doings."

"It's sad to find out that a good man has feet of clay, isn't it?" Doctor Vincent spoke softly as he picked up the reins, ready to drive back to the village.

"Yes, sir. But that doesn't keep me from loving him, even if my respect for him has diminished just a bit." She held up two fingers an infinitesimal piece apart. "Good day, Doctor. And thank you for coming."

"Take care, Miss Rebecca. Call if any of you need help." Off he went at a leisurely pace, his horse treated better than Cousin Ross' poor animal.

————

The next week, rain set in. An unusual event so late in summer. Breezes blew through windows and cooled the air. The rain washed the summer dust off bushes and rooftops. No need for watering flowers now. Mr. Gordon and Thomas spent the days inside, Thomas studying and the master gardener clarifying any questions he might have.

The household seemed to relax. Uncle Eugene and

Cousin Ross hadn't put in an appearance in almost two weeks. Rebecca's birthday was days away.

She sat at her desk in the office one morning as the rain fell heavier. No thunder. No lightning. Just a constant rain that had fallen for several days. The gas lights stayed on for most of the day. Hannah played with her dolls in the kitchen. Hattie dusted while Charlotte prepared dinner. Soon Hattie would go home. She came in the rain, and it looked like she would return in it. The same for Charlotte, though the cook wore a long, heavy raincoat like the coastal fishermen wore. A present from Mr. Gordon years ago.

Colleen wandered in, David asleep on her shoulder. "Can I sit with you for a little while? Maybe enjoy adult conversation. I've spent a great deal of time with David and Hannah and feel the need to speak longer words." She smiled when Rebecca nodded. Once seated, she eased the baby down onto her lap, head by her knees, bottom by her tummy. "He's growing so fast!"

"As are you. I hate to see you hide when visitors come. But for now, it's best."

"I understand. What are you working on?"

"Paying the latest bills I've received. Looking at the letters expressing interest in the jewels Papa left here. It seems there's a bidding war going on, though no one knows that but me. Still, I suppose all the jewel houses stay in contact with each other. So they are aware of who wants what and who has what."

"That's good for us, isn't it?"

"Yes, and no."

"How so?"

"Sooner or later, I have to deliver jewels to buyers. We can't ship them through the mail as if they're your Aunt

Fanny's letter. I'm hoping no one wants anything delivered until after my birthday. That way I can legally represent Gilpin and Company. Me being *the company*."

"I think Papa was incredibly farsighted to incorporate you into the business in such a way that you can seamlessly become the head of the company without him."

"I agree. However, when my big day is finally here and gone, we must post obituaries for Papa and Mama. Mama's can be local, but I must post Papa's in places like New York City, Chicago, Philadelphia, New Orleans, and San Francisco. Papa did business in all those towns. The businessmen need to know he's passed away, and the company still goes on."

"Won't someone ask who's running the company?"

"Probably. I'll answer them honestly and have the paperwork to back up my claim. Papa trained me in the business. He was also bonded. I'll have to get bonded as soon as I'm old enough."

"I never realized what you and Papa did here was that critical."

"Our future depends on what he taught me. Papa may have had feet of clay, as Doctor Vincent put it, but he was a realist. He knew he was of the older generation, and I was the younger. Obviously, I would outlive him. So he prepared me to take over the company."

"Smart man."

"No matter what we might think of him and his mistress, he was that...a farsighted, smart man."

"And he was loved."

"Amen."

———

Rebecca's birthday was such a celebration in spite of the rain, though the family kept it quiet. The family now included Thomas, of course. Hattie was already there and invited to share the fun. Because of the deaths in the family and the possible threat from the relatives, Rebecca celebrated her twenty-first birthday at home, surrounded by those who loved and cared for her. She wanted no gifts and told everyone so. But small, meaningful things found their way to her bedside table that morning and her desk at noon and beside her place at the birthday party, which was served as dessert after lunch.

"I am blessed to have such family and friends. Thank you all so very much. Now let's enjoy this beautiful cake that Charlotte made."

After lunch, Mr. Gordon drove her to the lawyer's office then the bank. By bedtime that night, she was officially twenty-one in the eyes of the law and rightful owner of Gilpin and Company and all that entailed.

Chapter 24
Three-Day Joke

A heavy hand hit the front door. Rain beat against the windows, making it hard to have a conversation, but no one could miss that pounding.

Rebecca motioned her sister to join her as she hastened to the foyer to see who was out on such a nasty night. The earlier rain of the day had turned into a deluge shortly after dark. Unless it was an emergency, no one should be out.

The door still locked, Rebecca turned up the gas light in the foyer. "Who's there?"

"Jonathan Murray from the village, miss. My misses and I moved into a house next to Hattie Johnson and her husband a couple of weeks ago. I wouldn't bother you, but her mister had an accident. His leg is hurt bad. Too bad to move. Mrs. Hattie sent me to fetch you. Said you could help."

"Me? Why me?"

"Said you were a calm person and would know what to do in an emergency. Her mister's too hurt to move. Can you come? She said to beg you if I had to. Breaks my heart to hear a woman sob like she'd doing."

"Poor Hattie. She must be scared out of her mind." Rebecca was already reaching for her cape and rain hat, but Colleen stayed her hand.

"Maybe you ought not go. You're an important person now. Even Hattie knows that. Besides, what can you do to help?"

"I have no idea, but if Hattie needs me and has begged me to come, I have to go, Colleen. I have to."

"Right. Be sure to wear your rubber boots. That rain is vicious. Bundle up well. Surely, you'll be back by morning."

"I hope so. I'll send someone if I can't come home shortly after dawn. By then, we should have done something to save Hattie's husband."

"You coming or not, miss?"

"Coming, Mr. Murray. Coming."

Holding the door so the wind wouldn't blow it open any more than necessary, Colleen kissed Rebecca's cheek and wished her luck.

The man took her arm and steadied her down the steps, out into the dark storm and into a large, enclosed carriage. Hands reached out for Rebecca. One hand went over her mouth while the other pulled her against a hard chest. Hands took a bandana and tied it across her mouth, silencing any chance she might have of screaming. Another bandana went across her eyes. Yet another pair of hands used rope to bind her wrists. Meanwhile, the man who escorted her to this dark hell apparently whipped the horses because the carriage lurched forward and moved out quickly.

Without a sense of time in solid darkness, knowing at least two people were with her, Rebecca almost gave way to tears. But she refused to cry unless the situation was hopeless. However brave that sounded in her mind, the rest of her trembled in abject terror. Once fear set in, she had no way to convince herself things would turn out all right.

She remembered being accidentally shut into the shed once when she was six. She'd sneaked in then fallen asleep. When she woke, she was alone, in the dark. Did anyone know where she was? Would anyone save her? Those same thoughts bounced through her mind.

No one knew who these men were. No one knew why they tied her up or raced off with her in the dark after telling a lie about going to Hattie Johnson's home. At least when morning came and no one could find her, Rebecca knew her family would start a search.

Until then, fear ate at her, despite the lack of tears. Beyond reason, she had no tears to shed because they remained bottled up inside her, watering her terror.

Sooner than she thought possible, the carriage stopped. She had no way of knowing where she was. She could still hear, however. But no one spoke. Someone manhandled her out of the carriage, not particularly careful about whether she slipped on the muddy steps or not. Her boots filled with mud as soon as she stood. Rain hit her head, uncovered, her hat somewhere in the carriage. She couldn't tell where she was. Couldn't hear anything. But she could smell something—manure, perhaps? A farm? Barn?

Hard hands held her arms and guided her into a shelter of some kind. Not a lot of protection against the wind until they entered another area. No wind. No rain. That was better. Try as she could though, she heard nothing. No animals—wild, domestic, or human.

Someone pushed her down, and she landed on her bottom in hay. She gathered a handful and pulled it up to smell it. Manure definitely, but this was old hay. Perhaps she was in a barn? But where?

Alone with no one holding her, she tried to stand. Hands came out of nowhere though and pushed her back down. A man growled at her, but she didn't recognize the voice. In the enclosed area, she could hear another man talking, but so low that again she couldn't recognize who spoke.

A carriage rolled into the area. Perhaps into the center aisle of the barn? The sound of harnesses and horses moving —into stalls?—came to her. Then silence. A rustling of hay. Another horse being led past her. Out into the rain, perhaps?

So many questions and no way to find answers. Frustration rivaled her fear, but fear raised its ugly head every time Rebecca thought she had an answer.

As the single horse passed her, going in the opposite direction from the others, she felt a stir of fresh air brush her cheek. *The horse is going outside. There has to be a rider with it.* She strained to hear a word, anything that might tell her who kidnapped her. She scooted forward until she hit a post. Probably the side of a stall. She bent her head as far as she could, afraid someone might catch her but needing information.

A whisper, a word here and there. What? What had she heard? A word...familiar...what was it? Rebecca racked her brain, trying to recall the word. With a silent scream, she recalled the word and recognized the voice.

Missy! Uncle Eugene!

Suddenly, fear turned to burning anger. How dare he! Cousin Ross couldn't be too far away. Two men were in the carriage with her. Her guts burned with a rage that, if ever turned loose, would make this storm seem tame.

Storm! Damn! Why do bad things happen when the weather is storming!

Knowing who took her calmed her nerves considerably, though she knew they could do despicable things to her before letting her go. Wait, who said they would let her go? Certainly not let her return to the family. She sank into deep thought. It seemed unlikely they would kill her. Colleen knew she went off to help the maid. Someone would come looking for her. Hopefully sooner rather than later. So why would they want her now?

Her head snapped up. The answer hit her so hard she groaned. They would hold her until after her birthday, then Ross would marry her. Together he and Uncle Eugene would carry her away, maybe across country or to Europe. Far enough away that no one could find her. Even if they did, she'd be married. Uncle would stay though, she reasoned. He would carry the marriage certificate back home, then do his best to demolish the Gilpin family.

Her mouth went into a straight line despite the gag. Her eyes squinted behind the blindfold. She had to escape.

Then she remembered. *Wait! My birthday was yesterday! Why are they kidnapping me today? I'm a free woman of commerce now. What happened that they should take me* after *my birthday?* Relieved at least to know her uncle and cousin would never be able to get their hands on the Gilpin money, knowing the girls and David would be safe even if something happened to her, she relaxed. Uncle didn't know about the will she left with the lawyer yesterday. That brought a smile to her gagged mouth. Knowing all that didn't ease the worry about escaping, however.

Without sight, it would be difficult, but she'd try. Listening, hearing nothing, she felt around her and determined she was indeed in a stall. Then she set about seeing how she might escape. The stall side boards were old. A few were loose, but the back wall was solid. Perhaps she could scoot through a broken board into another stall, then hide somewhere. It wasn't the best idea, but she might delay whatever plan her relatives had for her by a few minutes or hours while they searched for her. Anything to stall them would help.

Working fast in order to move from this area to another, she pushed a loose board at the back of the stall aside and wiggled through. Time was important now. With rain pounding the roof hard enough to make hearing difficult for her, she reasoned Uncle and Cousin would have as hard a time hearing her rustling around. Once she managed to gain the next stall over, she eased to her feet and felt along the far side.

She heard nothing but knew great risk often involved great danger. She had to move and move quickly. Barns usually had a ladder going to the upper loft. Maybe she could hide there...if she could find the ladder before the men discovered she wasn't where they left her. Risking discovery, she moved out of the stall and along the next one, following the sides until she came to yet another one. And another.

How big is this barn? Surely by now I'd have found a ladder or come to the doors.

Her hand hit something that wasn't a horizontal board but a vertical one...a ladder. Moving fast and trying to breathe through the gag, she put one foot, then another, on the rungs and began climbing.

Suddenly two hands jerked her off the ladder, sent her flying through the air until she landed hard on packed dirt. The fall knocked the breath out of her, and she gasped for air.

Rough hands pulled the gag out, and she fell back, sucking in air.

Alone on the floor, recovered but now angry all over again, she shouted. "Cowards! You sorry excuses for men! You worms! Kidnapping me for money! Sorry human beings! I name you cowards, Eugene and Ross Callaway."

With her eyes covered, she never saw the hand coming that slapped her almost unconscious. Her ears rang, and her head spun. She tasted blood on the side of her mouth. She spat, hoping the gob landed on one of them.

She sat up, wary of another attack. "Cowards."

"We might be, but we'll be rich ones soon enough. My man is riding to Philadelphia. When he returns in two days, he'll bring a judge with him. They are so easily bribed, you know. That man will marry you and Ross, and you two will disappear on a honeymoon that will last some time. After I manipulate my sister into a home for the mentally incompetent and waylay Robert, your sisters will be sent away, and I will claim the Gilpin fortune as a temporary guardian until my son returns with his bride. Which he won't. You will suffer a sad death, delivering a child. You and the child will die, leaving us wealthy."

"That's disgusting." Rebecca managed to get her hands and feet under her and stood, though she swayed without something to steady her. "No one will marry an unwilling woman."

"Your local minister and judges won't, that's true. But you will be willing, or your sisters will suffer accidents before you even say *I do*."

"You wouldn't!"

"Try me, Rebecca. I tried to be nice. Your father doesn't like me. I've known that for years. My sister is a weakling.

One not in good health. You told me so yourself. So what's to stop us? Humm?" Eugene positively gloated. His voice carried a satisfied tone that said he planned all this and now simply waited for events to fall into place.

"I won't marry Ross." She sounded as determined as possible. "And you will not take revenge on my sisters."

"And who's to stop me?"

"Oh, and I won't simply wait for Ross or one of your thugs to murder me in some far off land. I'll escape and return."

"Ooh, I'm scared." Now Eugene sounded plain sarcastic.

"You are a dead man, Eugene Callaway."

Her tone and words caught the attention of both men. She heard nothing, though she expected another slap. Or worse.

"Take her to a stall. Tie her up to a post. And put that gag back in her mouth. She's said enough." Eugene gave the order, but she felt sure Ross pulled her along, pushed her down and roughly tied her feet, then tied her body to a fat post.

That didn't go so well. Uncle—no, I won't call him that anymore—Eugene got a bit upset when I said I'd escape somehow and return to kill him. I'm not sure I can do that, the killing part, but I'm fairly sure I can escape. Ross has to sleep sometime. He thinks I'm simple anyway, enjoying lady books. Humm, maybe he doesn't think that anymore. After all, I just threatened to murder his father. Maybe I'll slip something nasty into Ross' coffee someday soon. Not enough to kill him but incapacitate him. Yes, that would work.

Happy with her plan—though how she would carry it out she had no idea—she managed to nap. No one stirred, so it seemed logical that in the storm, with her tied up, both men rested. Maybe one was on watch while the other slept, but both had their guards down.

Too bad she had no way to get loose. The new ropes held her tight. Bound like a turkey ready for the oven.

One thing about the blindfold was that she had no way to tell what time it was. Daylight? The middle of the night? If dawn came and Colleen didn't hear from Rebecca, her sister would check with Hattie. When that proved to be a false story, then Colleen would go to the police. Hopefully, she would tell them that she suspected her uncle and cousin of kidnapping.

Funny how lack of sight distorts the other senses. She had no way of knowing the time or if anyone was still around. She could be alone for all she knew, in a barn in the middle of nowhere. Perhaps a long way from home.

Her emotions went up then down then up again. She was sick with worry—for herself and her family. Eugene Callaway was mean enough to carry out his threats against the family if he didn't get what he wanted. Despite what could happen to her, he might hurt them anyway. Even before she cooperated. Which she didn't plan on doing.

Someone pulled off her gag and held a cup to her mouth. "Drink this." That was Ross. He sounded as nasty as his father did.

"Give me a minute for my mouth to work properly."

"Your mouth worked damn well last night. Now drink. It's the only one you may get." He removed the cup. "There. That's enough. Let's get this gag back on. I don't have any desire to listen to you threaten us again."

"Wait!"

"For what?"

"What time is it?"

"What do you care?"

"Please, what time is it?"

She heard him pop open a pocket watch. "Ten in the morning. So what?"

She sat silent. He squeezed her jaws until her mouth opened, and he replaced the gag.

With nothing else to do but worry, Rebecca spent a long day listening to what seemed to be a never-ending storm.

———

"Rebecca?"

That wasn't Ross or Eugene. She tilted her head and listened.

"Rebecca," the voice said again. Thomas! "We're here. Be still while I cut through this rope. Don't call attention to yourself. Ross and Eugene are at the other end of the barn. They mustn't suspect anything yet. The constables are on the way. We lost the carriage tracks and had to double back."

Thomas sawed through the ropes as he filled in Rebecca on her rescue. Boots approaching sent him scurrying away. Rebecca sat as she had with her loose hands behind her, still gagged and blindfolded.

"The judge should be here later today. We'll get this marriage over with, and you and Rebecca can take the carriage and meet the train. I've already secured tickets on a ship leaving New York for London."

"What am I going to do with a bride that hates me?" Ross's whining sounded like Hannah's when she was five.

"Throw her overboard if you want. I don't care, as long as I can secure that home and the money." Eugene must have given that statement more thought. "No, wait to dispose of her. I may need time to get rid of Robert and Felicity. The girls will be no problem. That old man and his wife can be paid off."

"If I have to," Ross whined again. Not an attractive feature in anyone, much less a man.

"You have to. Now let's get Rebecca up and cleaned up a bit. She may need to use the necessary too. Can't have her wetting herself in front of that judge." Eugene's laughter filtered through to Rebecca and turned her fear into anger again. She had no idea what Thomas and the others—whoever they were—had planned, so she would play along. But what about the cut ropes?

No sooner did Ross step into the stall than the men heard the sound of the double barrels of a shotgun click into place. That seemed to stop them in their tracks.

"You! You're an old man!" she heard Eugene say.

"I might be old, but I can blow your innards out pretty damn quick with this shotgun."

Mr. Gordon!

"Thomas, get Miss Rebecca up, and get that gag and blindfold off her."

Rebecca heard Thomas scurry behind her, slipping the gag out of her mouth and removing the blindfold. "Can you stand?"

"Give me a minute so my eyes can adjust." A few seconds and she nodded. Thomas helped her stand.

"We'll hold them here until the constables show up," Thomas said. "They're maybe thirty minutes behind us. We lost the carriage tracks. Lucky to find them at all in this storm, but Miss Colleen saw the carriage and knew no one in the village had a rig like that. By the time she got Thomas, herself, and me up in the buggy, we'd lost time. Then we had to backtrack. This place is in plain sight across a wide pasture, well off the road."

"You're telling me my sister is here?" Rebecca almost shrieked.

"Have you ever tried to stop Colleen from doing whatever she wanted?" Thomas supported Rebecca by the arm as she moved out of the stall. "Don't get close to them."

"No need to worry about that."

Suddenly Ross made a move for Rebecca, probably to use her as a shield so he and his father could escape before the law showed up. He grabbed her and attempted to pull her to his front, but she wasn't having any of it. She stomped his foot and swung around to land a blow on his ear.

Meanwhile, Eugene pulled a pistol from his pocket and attempted to make his way around Mr. Gordon. The old man wasn't having that either. He blew a hole in the side of the barn door with one barrel, stopping Eugene in his tracks. Infuriated, Eugene lifted his pistol and aimed for Mr. Gordon. At the same time, Rebecca landed her roundhouse punch. Ross grabbed Thomas as he fell, and both men stumbled back into the line of fire.

Eugene's pistol went off. Thomas and Ross fell.

"Thomas!" Rebecca and Mr. Gordon flew to the men. Eugene Callaway ran the other way, coward that he was, never checking to see if his son was hurt or not.

"Thomas!"

"Thomas, son. Are you all right?"

Thomas untangled himself from Ross and rolled away, blood on his shirtfront.

"Are you hurt?" Rebecca ran hands down his back and front, checking for wounds.

"I don't think so, but I think Ross might have taken that bullet meant for Mr. Gordon."

Rebecca turned to look at her cousin. Sure enough, he bled from a lower chest wound. His eyes were open, looking at her. Pain etched his features as tears slid down his cheeks.

"I'm hurt, Rebecca. Where's Father? I need him. I think I've been shot."

While it hurt her to see anyone injured as badly as Ross seemed to be, she couldn't find it in her heart to forgive him. His father had disappeared, leaving Ross to fend for himself.

"Miss Rebecca?" Mr. Gordon stood next to her. "Miss, you need to go see your sister. We made her stay in the buggy, but she's bound to have heard that shotgun blast and the pistol report. You know her, she'll be legging it up here any minute and see this fella if you don't stop her. Besides, it's not good for a lady in her condition to see this sort of thing."

"Right. Yes, you're right, Mr. Gordon. Colleen is just hardheaded enough to come running in here and do something like faint next to Ross." She held up a hand, and Mr. Gordon helped her stand. "Thomas, you and Mr. Gordon stay with Ross until the law shows up. They can carry him to Doctor Vincent."

"The doctor may not be able to help this kind of wound, Rebecca," Thomas said as he stood and moved to her side.

She nodded. She could feel no sympathy for her cousin. However, she did want to get to Colleen if for no other reason than to assure herself that Eugene or Ross did not harm her. Without knowing where Eugene Callaway went, he might have hurt her before he escaped if he saw her waiting the buggy.

Sure enough, she barely rounded the corner of the barn

door before she saw Colleen running toward the place. They met in a running hug, laughing and crying.

———

Back home, cleaned up, the family sat around the kitchen table drinking hot tea and retelling the tale of two crazy men and the kidnapping.

"Ross will never walk again. Doctor Vincent told Mr. Gordon that the bullet cut his spine. Eugene, of course, is long gone. I hate that the doctor is left to tell Ross that his father abandoned him to a life in someone else's care as an invalid." Rebecca shared the news about her cousin's injury without a shred of remorse. "I'm not coldhearted, but that's the way life is. They would have destroyed this family."

"Being an invalid is bad, but family to support the person helps more than you know," Charlotte said with a sniffle. She wiped her nose and let her husband explain.

"Charlotte's mom was an invalid in a chair most of her life. A barn rafter landed across her back, sort of like Ross. That never slowed that woman down, though. She accomplished almost everything she ever tried. I loved her as if she were my own mom."

"That's a wonderful story, Mr. Gordon. Thank you for sharing." Colleen sat with an empty lap as Thomas held David.

"What I don't understand," said Rebecca as she leaned forward over her cup, "is why they took me *after* my birthday. Surely they knew I was already legal and had no obligation to marry Ross or turn over money to them."

"Oh, I can answer that." Colleen grinned and patted her sister. "Ross asked me a long time ago what day your birthday was. I told him three days later than the real date. I was just playing with him, but he remembered. They didn't know you had already gone to the lawyer and bank when they took you."

"Oh, sister!" Rebecca got up, pulled Colleen to her feet and hugged her so hard that Colleen gurgled.

"You're smushing me. Give over, Rebecca."

"Smushing? That's a new word, I think." Rebecca let Colleen sit, but laughed at her. "Very creative, sister."

"Thank you, Madam Company President," returned Colleen.

"How would you like to be vice president?"

Colleen gave that offer about two seconds of thought before declining. "I think my talents lie in other directions, Rebecca." She cut a shy glance at Thomas who didn't see it. "But I thank you anyway."

"Family, I think we can now let the world know that Papa and Mama are gone. And we can officially adopt our brother. Is there anything else we need to do?" Rebecca sounded like the president of a company, and she felt it suited her well.

Hannah held up her hand. "I think we're going to be all right, sister."

"I won't even put that to a vote. I do believe Miss Hannah has the right of it. We shall now get on with our lives and live them as if each day matters, for each one does."

"And we'll make logical decisions and hope they stay that way," added Hannah.

"Amen, sister. Amen." Rebecca and Colleen blessed their sister's words.

Chapter 25
A Year and a Half Later

Rebecca stepped down from the buggy and waved the new man, Marshall, on to the barn. Before her stood home, welcoming her with the sweet smell of flowers. She picked up her valise and moved to the steps.

Funny how everything looks the same, but isn't, she thought. *Coming home feels so good. I wonder if that's how Papa felt when he returned.*

"Rebecca! Rebecca!" Hannah must have heard the buggy and saw her from the upstairs window. "You're home. I'm coming down!"

As she moved up to the door, all she heard was Hannah shouting and the thunder of boots on the staircase. She threw open the door and immediately fell into her little sister's embrace.

"I missed you so much, but we had so much fun. I made an A on my spelling test, and Jimmy only made a B. Mrs. Gordon made a cake for us, and we ate it outside on the lawn." Hannah's chatter stopped when a little boy came running to meet his sister.

"Becca! Becca!" He threw his arms around her legs, then held up his arms. "Want up! Now!"

"Demanding little man, aren't you?" She reached down, scooped up the little one and swung him in a circle, then squeezed him to her as hard as she possibly could. But only for a second. David Gilpin wanted to be held, but for only a second. His life was just too active to stay still any longer than that.

"Rebecca!" Colleen ran in from the kitchen and threw herself into Rebecca's arms. "You've been gone ever so long! I missed you!"

"I think she exaggerates, Rebecca." Thomas followed Colleen in, carrying William, Colleen's son.

"I do not exaggerate!" She reached for her son, but her son reached for his Aunt Rebecca. "Well, I can tell when I'm not wanted." She started to turn away in jest, but Thomas pulled her to his side.

"I've only been gone a week, ladies and gentlemen. I missed all of you as well." She nuzzled the baby as she took a seat on the staircase. David immediately sat beside her, his elbow resting on her knee. William sat in her lap. "So how's life here? Where's Charlotte? And Hattie?"

"Charlotte is outside helping Hattie hang some big sheets. She'll be back in shortly. Only a dead man could miss you returning home." Colleen coaxed her son from his aunt's lap and cuddled him, which made him laugh.

"And what about you, Thomas?"

"When this semester is done, so am I."

"I had no idea you were so close to finishing college," she applauded, to which he bowed. "And what are your plans for after you finish?"

Before he could answer, Charlotte flew into the foyer. "Miss Rebecca, we missed you."

Rebecca laughed but stood and hugged the woman, now looking older. She remembered starting the trips over a year ago, with Mr. Gordon driving her to the village to catch the train. Peter Gordon was gone now, passing away peacefully in his chair on the front porch of his home just beyond the trees.

Hattie passed through the hall with an armload of fresh sheets. "Welcome home, Miss Rebecca. We missed you. Coming through." She waited for everyone to move aside so she could go upstairs to make up the beds.

"*Welcome home* sounds so good." Rebecca looked around at those who loved and cared for her and felt blessed.

———

"Walk with me, Hannah?" Rebecca held out one hand to her little sister.

"Where to?"

"I thought we'd visit Mama and Papa and Peter."

"Let me get my hat."

Hannah returned with her hat and one for her sister. Instead of holding hands as they used to, Rebecca slipped Hannah's arm through hers.

"You're getting so tall. I hadn't realized it until just now."

"I'm not little anymore."

"No, miss, you are not."

Together they walked across the lawn and to the back of the property, to the area that Peter Gordon had made into a family cemetery. Little did he know he would one day be buried there, considered part of the Gilpin family. Not far from the family plot was a small cross showing where Rags the dog now laid.

Rebecca brushed oak leaves off Mama's gravestone while Hannah did the same to Papa's. She gently cleaned off Peter's stone, then straightened the cross over the dog's grave.

"It's peaceful here. I'm glad I came," Rebecca said with a contented sigh.

"Was it hard?" Hannah asked after a moment.

"What, sweeting?"

"Writing that for the papers last year? About Mama and Papa. I wanted to ask then, but you looked so sad."

"The obituaries, you mean?"

Hannah nodded.

"Yes, it was, but I kept them simple. I did lie about Papa's death a little, saying he died while on a business trip. That was near enough to the truth. And Mama's was the truth... she died of illness. She really had been ill. The news about Papa just made it worse very fast."

"Colleen said you had to put Papa's obituary in a lot of newspapers."

"That's right. Papa did business all over the United States. Those he dealt with had to know. It was my responsibility, and those notices made it easier for me to conduct business. The men knew Papa was no longer available, and I was the owner and head of the company."

"Was it hard to work with them? Men can be hard sometimes."

"My goodness, young miss. Wherever did you get that idea?"

"Jimmy Connelly. He's ever so hard to deal with."

Rebecca kept her laugher in check for fear of hurting her sister's feelings. "A few of the men did indeed expect to deal with another man, but they changed their minds eventually."

"Because you're so beautiful and smart."

"I think it's maybe because I am good at my business, young lady."

Hannah patted Peter's gravestone and stood, brushing leaves off her skirt. "Mr. Marshall is doing well, but he's not like Mr. Gordon. He doesn't laugh like Mr. Gordon did." Hannah closed the gate to the little cemetery.

"Perhaps Marshall hasn't quite found his place in the family yet. Give him time."

"Time gets away from us sometimes, doesn't it?"

"I think you're right. Hannah. We go along in our lives, thinking we have tomorrow, and then we don't."

"We need to make the most of each day, don't we, sister?"

"Too true, little one. Too true."

———

That evening found the family—including Thomas and Charlotte, who now lived with the girls—in the family parlor. No one but family ever came in there anymore. Strangers met the family in the drawing room.

The windows stood open. A light springtime breeze ruffled curtains, and each person sat doing what they enjoyed the most. Hannah read. Colleen played with William, and Thomas entertained David. Charlotte knitted while Rebecca sat watching them all, a letter in her hand.

"Thomas, I never heard what you plan on doing when you finish college." She turned to him and sat comfortably in her chair waiting for the answer she never got earlier that day.

"The Division of Forestry was founded in 1881.

Congress passed the Forest Reserve Act in 1891. With my interest and degree in agriculture, I plan on joining that service. I've already talked to the man in charge of this area, and he will station me here."

"That's wonderful. When you and Colleen marry this summer, you will continue to live here. Well, in this house instead of the Gordon's home. Is that all right with you?"

"That's perfect." Thomas gave Rebecca such a smile that she knew he hoped his plans would allow him to remain part of the family here.

"What will happen if he is transferred to another station?" Colleen glanced at Thomas but focused on William and David. "What will David do without his little nephew? They are so close in age that they might miss each other terribly."

"Colleen, now, we agreed not to worry about this unless it happens...someday." Thomas put his hand on her shoulder.

"I know. I know. But I do worry. I've raised David from an infant. I'd miss him as much as William."

"Colleen," Rebecca paused, hoping her words would soothe her sister's worry. "If your family gets transferred, may we deal with David at that time? I think we can work out something satisfactory."

"Will that leave you, me, and Charlotte if Colleen and Thomas and the boys leave?" Hannah wore an inquiring look on her face, not a worried anxious one.

"Well, I suppose if that day comes then yes, that will leave the three of us. We can manage, can't we ladies?"

"Aye, we can." Charlotte winked at first Hannah and then Rebecca.

While Colleen and Thomas settled the boys on their laps and Hannah showed Charlotte a picture in the book she was reading, Rebecca savored the pleasures of home and sharing family news. Speaking of which...

"I have a letter from the private investigator I hired a year ago. About Eugene Callaway. Would you like to hear it? I think it will lay to rest our concerns about him."

The family turned to her, expectation on some faces, a hint of fear on others.

"Yes, please. I hope he's stuck in some hole and can't get out," Colleen muttered in a vicious tone.

"Miss Colleen, that's no way for a lady to speak!" Charlotte should have been immune to Colleen's comments by now, but that never prevented the good woman from reminding the middle daughter how to act properly.

"But then she's no lady," Rebecca stuck her tongue out at Colleen at which everyone laughed.

"Well, read on then, ye of stuck-out tongue." Colleen did a bow from a sitting waist and waved her hand graciously for Rebecca to proceed.

Miss Gilpin,

Per our agreement, I finally located Eugene Callaway after a number of near misses in at least a dozen states out west. However, I was too late to bring him to your justice. It seems the locals did that.

After kidnapping you, threatening your family, and shooting his son, Callaway ran. He stole a horse and rode away, which is why we never found a trace of him by train or coach. He finally stopped several months back outside San Francisco, California. He created a con wherein he sold land that he did not own but belonged to a man living out of state. He sold the land for several thousands of dollars each to five different men who lived near San Francisco. By chance, none of the men visited the property at the same time, a risk Callaway was willing to take.

The owner's neighbor, who looked after the property, finally met one of the buyers. He contacted the real owner immediately. When the police showed up at Callaway's boarding house, the man carried only a hundred dollars and loudly proclaimed his innocence.

The police took him to the local jail to be seen by the judge the next day. Meanwhile, the men who had been bilked out of their entire savings in several cases stormed the police station but could not get to Callaway.

Not until the next day was it discovered that one of the men committed suicide, having spent his family's entire savings, leaving them almost destitute.

When the police left the station to cross the street, with Callaway handcuffed between them, a young man rapidly approached, pulled out a small pistol, and shot Callaway. The boy's father was the one who killed himself. Callaway did not survive his wound. He lies in a pauper's grave in Orange Cemetery outside San Francisco. The police have yet to recover the money he swindled from the families.

Regards,
  Levin York
  York and Even Detective Agency

"That's the most extraordinary story I've ever heard." Thomas shook his head. "I can only imagine how he felt when he left. Later Callaway must have thought himself safe enough to start a swindle like that. And the money is still missing. Ross could use that, poor man."

No one had any other comments, even Colleen.

Rebecca folded the letter carefully and slipped it back into the envelope. "That settles that concern. Eugene Callaway will never bother this family again. Nor will his son."

With the family in a bit of a gloomy mood, she intentionally let slip an interesting piece of news that she'd kept to herself for several months now. "I met an interesting gentleman while traveling."

Everyone swiveled their heads her way, their mouths open like landed fish.

Colleen gave her sister a suspicious glare. "Really? And when did you plan on telling us this?"

"I'm telling you now, aren't I?"

"And just how long have you known this interesting gentleman?"

"Oh, maybe six months. You see, we met at a trade show. We tend to travel to the same cities and same jewelers. We started talking, and one thing led to another."

"And what is this *one thing* and *another*? And what is his name, for God's sake?" The family seemed content to let Colleen interrogate Rebecca, but they all seemed to enjoy watching the oldest sister squirm a little.

"Collin Devereux. He's from New Orleans but travels to the same places I do. We actually started coordinating our schedules so we can meet more often." Rebecca tried to maintain an innocent expression but wanted to laugh watching the others.

"And so?"

"So we might travel to New Orleans after Colleen and Thomas' wedding to meet his family. And look for jewels to sell, of course."

"Oh, of course." Colleen threw up one hand, the other

one holding her son. "And when does he come here to meet *your* family?"

"I believe that would be just *before* your wedding. He will be my guest."

"This is serious, Rebecca?"

"I...I think it could be."

"Well, I for one hope you find great happiness with this Collin Devereux, Miss Rebecca." Charlotte blew her a kiss from across the room.

"Me too. I hope he's nice." Hannah wore an ever so slight frown of concern.

"He's a delightful man, dear, and he's so anxious to meet all of you. But I think he's afraid you won't like him."

Colleen rolled her eyes up and sat with a mouth cocked to one side. "Oh, now really. The man can't be that silly. Of course, we'll like him."

"Changed your tune there, have you?" Thomas teased, and she had the courtesy to blush.

"Well, yes. I only want Rebecca to be as happy as I am."

"That's sweet, my dear. And for that, I'm giving you a little kiss right here in front of the family."

Colleen would have pushed him away, as a kiss here wouldn't be appropriate, but Thomas was too fast and kissed her forehead. She swatted him but leaned into him, her love evident.

"Our family is growing and seems happy to do so." Rebecca sighed, for the family could have received her news badly. Fortunately, that wasn't the case.

"That's a logical statement." Hannah came to snuggle in Rebecca's lap.

"I think it is."

"I don't think we'll see any illogical consequences for that one."

"I think you're right, sweetheart." Rebecca kissed Hannah's forehead and snuggled her closer. "I think you're absolutely right."

———

Let me hear from you if you enjoyed this story
about young ladies caught up in troubles.
janer.carver@gmail.com

———

Don't miss out on your next favorite book!

Join the Melange Books mailing list at
www.melange-books.com/mail.html

THANK YOU FOR READING

Did you enjoy this book?

We invite you to leave a review at the website of your choice, such as Goodreads, Amazon, Barnes & Noble, etc.

DID YOU KNOW THAT LEAVING A REVIEW...

- Helps other readers find books they may enjoy.
- Gives you a chance to let your voice be heard.
- Gives authors recognition for their hard work.
- Doesn't have to be long. A sentence or two about why you liked the book will do.

About the Author

A varied life for me—student, teacher, wife, mom, writer, editor, quilter and an adventurer when possible. My goal? Do something outrageous every day. Doesn't always happen, but I try.

Jane also writes young adult fiction under the name Jane Grace. Find her books at our YA imprint, Fire & Ice Young Adult Books.

www.romances-by-janie.com
www.JaneGracePresents.com

Also by Jane Carver

Novels

Return With Honor

The Answer Key

The Gilpin Girls

Short Stories

Winning the Ranger's Heart, featured in *Western Ways*